"I DO FIND YOU INTRIGUING," ASHLEY admitted softly.

"And I find you equally so," Eric said. "But we are going to resist that feeling, yes?" Nevertheless, he reached behind her head and began removing the pins holding her hair in a sophisticated twist.

"Resist," she repeated breathlessly, mesmerized by the way he worked his mouth as he concentrated on his task.

He combed his fingers through her hair until it all fell loosely to her shoulders, tugging slightly until she moaned and melted against him. He kissed her then, his mouth capturing her lips with masterful force.

Ashley shivered with pleasure and surprise. She'd been wrong. Anticipation hadn't prepared her for this moment. The feel of his lips on hers was all she'd dreamed of and more. He was strong, yet gentle, possessive, yet giving. "Oh, yes," she sighed against his mouth. "Yes."

Eric felt her nails press against his back, tingly sensations skittering down his spine. Her bracelets jingled near his ear, and the music of a thousand centuries played through his body, a song of need and desire. When she opened her mouth to him, he took all that was offered, and more. . . .

WHAT ARE *LOVESWEPT* ROMANCES?

They are stories of true romance and touching emotion. We believe those two very important ingredients are constants in our highly sensual and very believable stories in the LOVESWEPT line. Our goal is to give you, the reader, stories of consistently high quality that may sometimes make you laugh, sometimes make you cry, but are always fresh and creative and contain many delightful surprises within their pages.

Most romance fans read an enormous number of books. Those they truly love, they keep. Others may be traded with friends and soon forgotten. We hope that each LOVESWEPT romance will be a treasure—a "keeper." We will always try to publish

LOVE STORIES YOU'LL NEVER FORGET
BY AUTHORS YOU'LL ALWAYS REMEMBER

The Editors

Loveswept ® 689

NO PROMISES MADE

MARIS SOULE

BANTAM BOOKS

NEW YORK · TORONTO · LONDON · SYDNEY · AUCKLAND

NO PROMISES MADE

A Bantam Book / May 1994

*If you would be interested in receiving protective vinyl covers for your
Loveswept books, please write to this address for information:*

*Loveswept
Bantam Books
P.O. Box 985
Hicksville, NY 11802*

ISBN 0-553-44336-4

Published simultaneously in the United States and Canada

Bantam Books are published by Bantam Books, a division of Bantam Dou-
bleday Dell Publishing Group, Inc. Its trademark, consisting of the words
"Bantam Books" and the portrayal of a rooster, is Registered in U.S. Patent
and Trademark Office and in other countries. Marca Registrada. Bantam
Books, 1540 Broadway, New York, New York 10036.

PRINTED IN THE UNITED STATES OF AMERICA

OPM   0 9 8 7 6 5 4 3 2 1

Dedicated to the memory of
Professor Law,
whose dojo was a place
for learning and growth.

Also, my thanks to
Ann Hooghart,
for helping me understand
the Japanese culture.

ONE

Ashley Kehler couldn't find her underwear. Which wasn't all that unusual for her. She was always losing things, at least temporarily. Her brother Jack used to tell her it was because she was a blonde. Back then, when she'd been a child, she'd believed him. Now, she knew it was because she always tried to do too many things at once.

What bothered her tonight was that she hadn't taken her lingerie out of the dryer more than five minutes ago. It should be in her basket, but it wasn't.

Hands on her hips, she turned slowly, visually checking every shelf and countertop in the basement. She had to have laid her things down somewhere.

A disgruntled sigh expressed her frustration.

"Problems?" asked Charlie Iler, the retired widower who managed the apartment building, as he came down the stairs.

"I've lost it," Ashley said. She lifted her hands in defeat. "I need a keeper."

"Well, I've been telling you a pretty little thing like you needs a husband." Charlie grinned. His broad smile and round, nearly bald head always reminded her of *Peanuts'* Charlie Brown. Charlie Iler, however, was a lot more savvy than Charlie Brown. Little ever got by him.

Ashley went back to her search. Just in case she'd absentmindedly mixed her underwear in with her linens, she dug through the sheets and towels she'd just folded and set in her basket. Her hands, with their gold rings and long, well-manicured nails, moved quickly, skimming over each piece. "What I need is to get organized, Charlie. Then maybe I wouldn't be doing my laundry at ten o'clock at night when I have to get up at five in the morning."

"What you need to do, young lady, is slow down," he chastised. "Every time I see you, you're in a hurry. Always running here and there."

She laughed amiably at his suggestion. "In public relations you don't make it to the top by going slow." And she had an important presentation at eight o'clock the next morning. Since she was wearing her last pair of everything, she really needed to find her underwear.

It wasn't in her basket.

"You met your new neighbor yet?" Charlie asked, crossing over to his workbench near the furnace.

"No, but I can hear his music through the wall between our apartments." She glanced Charlie's way. She and all the other tenants were always complaining about the apartment building's paper-thin walls. Not that Charlie could do much about it. He simply managed the building. Some Detroit lawyer who rarely came to Ann Arbor owned the place.

"Weird-sounding stuff, ain't it?" Charlie shook his head and began rummaging through a drawer of his workbench.

"Sounds Oriental to me." And she didn't particularly like the high-pitched, twangy sound.

"Probably is. Guess he's what you'd call Amerasian. Said his father's American, his mother's Japanese, and he's lived half of his life in Japan." Charlie pulled out a couple of washers. "His name's Eric Newman."

Eric Newman. She remembered that Jack had once had a friend named Eric. A very close friend. It seemed so long ago.

Ashley chased the memory away.

"He got a package from Japan yesterday," Charlie went on. "He was out, so they left it with me. Had all those funny characters on it, and in English it was addressed to Newman-*sensei*. Any idea what that means?"

"None whatsoever." What Charlie was saying, however, did give her an idea. "Maybe I could get him to teach me some Japanese. With so many Japanese companies coming into Michigan, it wouldn't hurt."

"Sounds good." Charlie smiled, then turned his back to her and began digging through a toolbox. "By the way, he's a ninja warrior."

"A what?" Ashley wasn't sure she'd heard him correctly.

"Ninja." He straightened and faced her, a long-handled wrench in his hand. "That's what some guy who came to see him told me. A real live ninja warrior."

"Oh, great." Just what they needed. So far the building's tenants included a psychologist who analyzed everything anyone said; a poet who recited his poetry in the stairwell; a pair who were Ann Arbor's answer to the odd couple; and a male stripper who kept offering to let her watch him practice for free. Why not add a ninja warrior? "He's not one of those turtles, is he?"

"Naw." Charlie chuckled. "Least I didn't see any shell on his back." Wrench and washers in hand, he headed back toward the stairs. "That party of yours starting at nine Friday night?"

"There or about. You are coming, aren't you?"

"If I can keep this darn building from falling down around us, I'll be there." He stopped at the stairway and tapped the wrench against a cardboard box by the bottom step. "If you're looking for some frilly things, you might find 'em in here."

Of course. The moment Charlie said it, Ashley remembered. She'd been looking at one of the magazines another tenant had left in the box when the buzzer for the dryer had gone off. She'd had the magazine with her when she'd gotten her underwear. Just as she was going to put the magazine back, the buzzer on the other dryer had sounded.

"Thanks, Charlie," she called after him as he went up the stairs.

"Any time." He paused, looking back down at her, and grinned. "He's not married."

And Charlie was playing matchmaker. She laughed lightly and shook her head. "I'm not looking."

"Yeah, right." He chuckled and went on up the stairs.

She wasn't looking, but that didn't mean she couldn't be hospitable. Laundry basket perched on her hip, Ashley stood in front of the door to Eric Newman's apartment. She could hear music playing on the other side. She could also hear a thumping sound. Hesitantly, she knocked.

The thumping stopped immediately. Putting on a friendly smile, she mentally rehearsed her next-door-neighbor-stopping-by-to-say-hello greeting. The moment the door opened, however, she was speechless.

Almond-shaped eyes as dark as the night and as clear as the heavens locked onto hers, the intensity of his gaze taking her breath away. She felt as though he were looking right into her soul, stripping her bare of every ounce of confidence and poise she'd carefully honed over her twenty-seven years of life.

It was only when his gaze moved down her body that her mind began to function again. Yet even then it wasn't logic that spun through her mind, but rapid-fire impressions, feelings, sensations. . . .

Of height, though the man wasn't tall. Maybe five-ten or -eleven.

Of strength. Not a muscle-your-way-through-life kind of strength, but an animal grace. A durability. An inner strength.

And of danger.

Emotional danger.

Something curled in her stomach, and her legs felt weak. Just looking at him, she knew this man was different from others she'd met in her lifetime. It was more than his unusual and striking half-American, half-Japanese features. More than the confident, self-assured way he was staring at her. An aura surrounded him, a magnetism that held her spellbound.

Everything he wore was black, from his loose-fitting canvas jacket—cinched by a long, heavy, double-wrapped cloth belt—to his baggy trousers, to his single-toed footwear. Even his hair was black, and his eyes were as dark a brown as she'd ever seen.

Ninja. The word echoed in her mind.

Here was a man who possessed secrets known to only a few. A man of potential violence, savagery.

Here also was a man who would interest her.

Quickly, she shook off that thought. This was not the time to be getting interested in anyone. She had a goal to reach, promises to fulfill, and that meant forgetting men or romance. For now, at least.

Still, she couldn't stop the shiver that ran down her spine or the sudden quickening in her pulse.

"Are you all right?" he asked, his voice deeper than she'd expected, throatier. "You look flushed."

"I'm fine." Except she sounded breathless. "I must have come up the stairs too quickly."

It was possible, she thought. Her mouth was ridiculously dry, and her heart was racing much too fast. Yes, it had to be the stairs.

Only she couldn't remember feeling this way before he opened the door.

"You have been doing your laundry."

It was a statement, not a question, and they both glanced at the basket balanced on her hip. To her dismay she realized her underwear lay on top—lacy, frilly panties and bras that showed how much and how little she wore under her clothes each day.

His gaze came back to her face. "I have not been down to the basement yet. I hate doing laundry."

"So do I," she admitted, and managed a smile. She had a feeling he was trying to put her at ease, verbally soothing her tensed nerves. She chided herself for not dropping her basket of clothes off at her apartment first. On the other hand, it did make her visit seem more spontaneous. "I'm your next-door neighbor, Ashley Kehler."

She held out her right hand, and he took it in both of his, bowing slightly. "Pleased to meet you, Ashley Kehler. I am Eric Newman."

"I know." Without thinking, she bowed her head, too, feeling strangely hesitant and demure. It wasn't a feeling she liked. One of her father's favorite sayings was that it was the take-charge person who held the advantage. The way she was feeling, she needed an advantage.

Slipping her hand free, she looked Eric straight in the eyes. "Charlie Iler was downstairs just a few minutes ago. He was telling me a bit about you."

"Ah, the apartment-building manager." Eric nodded, the touch of a smile curving his mouth. "He has been telling me a bit about you, also."

Knowing Charlie, Ashley could imagine what he'd said—that she worked too hard and needed a man. In fact, the way Charlie was always trying to match her up with someone, he'd probably already suggested to Eric that he take her out.

The thought made her cringe inside, and she hoped it wasn't true. "You can't always believe everything Charlie tells you."

Eric's eyebrows rose slightly. "Should I believe you are in public relations?"

"Well, yes. I'm with Stedfeld's."

She paused, waiting to see if he showed any recognition of the company's name. He didn't, so she went on. "It's a large Chicago-based PR firm that has branches throughout the Midwest, including Ann Arbor. I'm a director."

"I see."

She wondered what he did see. His gaze darted to her hair, to her gold earrings, and to her mouth, leaving her feeling oddly uncomfortable. Without thinking, she reached up to feel if her twist was still holding and licked her lips, then wished she hadn't. He noticed that too.

He smiled. "Charlie also said that you worked long hours. You must. It is late to be doing laundry."

"It sort of got away from me." She wondered if there was another message he was trying to convey. "I hope it wasn't too late to stop by. I wouldn't have, but I heard the music and noises coming from your apartment and figured you were still up."

"No, it is not too late. I was doing my *kata* to the *koto*."

She looked beyond him into his apartment, just able to see the edge of a black leather couch and a low red coffee table. "What's a *kata* and a *koto*?"

"*Kata* are sets of moves. Sort of a choreographed sequence of martial-arts forms. The *koto* is the Japanese harp."

"That's a harp?" She knew she was wrinkling her nose, but the instrument she could hear certainly didn't sound like a harp.

"You do not like it?"

Her tone and facial expression certainly had said as much, and since the night before his music had had her ready to scream, honesty overruled politeness. "Not really."

"Not really," he repeated, and chuckled.

"I mean, it's different. It's just that I find the sound sort of twangy."

"Ah, twangy." Again he chuckled. "You prefer the screeching and bellowing of opera, I take it."

Obviously, he'd heard her stereo that morning. "I'm sorry. I had it too loud, didn't I? I'm trying to cultivate an appreciation for opera." Not too successfully, she was afraid. "I didn't think about it bothering you. These walls are so damn thin. We've all complained about it. With Mr. Bernstein, the man who used to live in your apartment, I never worried about making noise. He was half-deaf."

"In Japan, all apartments have thin walls. I have learned to block out extraneous noises."

"Usually, I listen to soft rock." Not that it mattered, she realized. What they were discussing was volume, not personal tastes. "I'll keep my music turned down."

"And so will I."

"Except this Friday night," she went on, "I'm afraid the music and noise may get loud then. You have heard about the party, haven't you?" She didn't wait for his answer. "I've invited people from work, friends, and everyone in the apartment building. If you haven't heard about it, you're invited too. It starts at nine. Dress is casual."

"Charlie said something about a party the other day." Gazing at her face—at her mouth—Eric seemed to consider the idea; then he shook his head. "No, it would not be wise."

"Would not be wise?" His answer surprised and disappointed her. "And why would it 'not be wise'?"

"Because . . ." He hesitated and ran a hand through his hair. She watched his long, slender fingers part the thick strands, and for a moment she could imagine the feel of his hair, could sense its vibrancy and warmth. His words brought her back to reality.

"I cannot come because I have paperwork to do," he said. "I am opening a dojo—a martial-arts training school—and I have discovered that the state of Michigan requires a lot of paperwork. Reams of it."

She understood paperwork. She certainly had her share at work and often brought it home. She also understood the quiet one needed to do paperwork. Either Eric was simply making excuses, or he didn't have any idea how big a party this was going to be.

"There will be a lot of people here," she said. "Maybe a hundred, if everyone shows up. From nine o'clock on, this place is going to be jumping. I don't think you're going to get a lot of work done."

"Jumping." He laughed once more, the sound deep and melodious.

"Do come," she urged. "Take a break from your work. I'm sure you'd have a good time."

He started to say something, then stopped himself and again shook his head.

His reticence intrigued her. Here she was offering free booze and food, only a few steps away from his door. Then she thought of a reason for his hesitation. "Look, no matter what Charlie's told you, I'm really not a man-hungry woman on the prowl for a husband."

"He did not say you were."

"Well, I'm surprised he didn't. I mean, he's always telling me I need to get married, that I need a man. I just wanted you to know, if that's what you've heard, it's Charlie's idea, not mine."

"You are not interested in men?" Eric asked, his eyebrows rising.

"No, I don't mean that. It's just that I have to make it to Chicago first."

"Ah."

She didn't ask what he meant by that. She was getting in too deep as it was. And why she cared if he came to her party or not, she didn't know.

She was tired. That was it. In the morning Eric Newman would be just another man. In the light of a new day she wouldn't care whether he came to her party or worked on papers, wouldn't care what Charlie had or hadn't told him, or that Eric Newman had the most entrancing eyes she'd ever seen.

Unable to pull her gaze from those eyes, she slowly backed up. "Well, nice meeting you."

"Nice meeting you." He nodded politely, almost formally, but he never looked away from her face.

She didn't go far. She knew sleep might give her a better perspective, but there was no way Eric Newman would ever be just another man. Everything about him was intriguing. His looks, his almost Oriental way of speaking—though without a trace of an accent—his occupation. "Are you really a ninja?"

"I will be teaching ninjutsu at my dojo, if that is what you mean. Along with karate, judo, and other forms of martial art. Are you interested?"

"Oh, no. I don't like violence . . . and besides, I don't have time for anything like that." Especially not now. It was just that from the moment he'd opened his door, she'd felt mesmerized . . . somehow under his power. There had to be a reason. "I read somewhere that ninjas can hypnotize others. Is that true?"

Just the hint of a smile touched his mouth. "A ninja learns to use the power of suggestion."

What suggestions was he giving her? Why couldn't she simply turn away and walk to her apartment?

"Could I learn how to use that power of suggestion so some people—specifically a screening committee—will think I'm the best person for a position?"

He studied her without speaking, and she waited. It seemed an eternity before he nodded slightly. "I believe you already have the power."

If so, it was a surprise to her. "I wish."

She did manage one more step back before he stopped her with another question. "And are you the best?"

"Yes," she said without hesitation. At least she was

sure she was the best qualified for the position she wanted. In fighting this sudden attraction she felt, however, she was a complete failure.

"Then you will succeed."

His words warmed her from the inside out. Or maybe it was his smile. She wasn't sure of anything anymore. "Don't forget, after you finish your paperwork Friday night, come on over. It's going to be a great party."

"I am sure it will be."

She did manage to turn away and head for her apartment, but at her door, she looked back. He was still watching her. Just for good measure, she added, her tone quite serious, "You know what they say about all work and no play. . . ."

She paused for effect but didn't give him a chance to answer. With a laugh she finished. "They say it's no fun. See you Friday night."

Eric didn't move until Ashley had closed her door; then he let out his breath and slowly stepped back into his apartment.

Fun.

It had been quite a while since he'd done anything purely for fun. His decision to move to Ann Arbor had kept him too busy the last few months for playtime, and it had been ages since he'd had fun in the company of a woman.

Maybe too many ages for a healthy thirty-four-year-old body. His male hormones had certainly reacted to Ashley Kehler.

What surprised him was, so had his mind.

From Charlie's description of her he hadn't thought he would be interested. Perhaps it had been wrong, but the moment Charlie had said she was a petite, blue-eyed blonde, he'd stereotyped her. And when he'd first seen those long fingernails and the three gold rings she wore, he had imagined she was an airhead, who could spend hours primping and priming; a woman in search of a man to keep her in the manner she'd like to become accustomed to.

The longer she'd talked to him, though, the more he'd realized that Ashley Kehler was more than pink nail polish, gold rings, long lashes, and the scent of an expensive perfume. More than honey-colored hair pulled back in a sophisticated twist.

After a few minutes the only thing he'd known for certain was that Ashley *was* petite, the top of her head coming just to his chin, and that she had the most delectably enticing mouth he had ever seen. More than once, he'd caught himself wondering what it would be like to kiss her, how her mouth would feel against his, how she would taste.

Crazy thoughts, for certain, for a man who was going to be swamped with work over the next few months. A man whose capital was tied up in property and equipment. A man whose lifestyle and beliefs didn't appeal to most women—let alone a woman who was in public relations. Her job involved being in the limelight, making news, getting noticed. He'd been trained to work in secret, in the dark.

He closed his eyes and pictured Ashley's face. Her finely etched features gave her a delicate, almost fragile look, while her eyes were so blue, they'd sparkled like pools of deep water. She was pretty, all right, and even though the baggy sweatsuit she'd had on had camouflaged her figure, he didn't doubt Charlie's word that Ashley had a great body.

Pretty, intelligent, and just his opposite.

As far as Eric could see, what he needed to do was stay as far away from Ashley Kehler as possible. Ignore his physical needs. Forget that enticing mouth.

Which meant he'd better do his paperwork at his dojo on Friday night. Otherwise, he just might be tempted to go to her party.

The lady was too appealing. Too damned appealing.

TWO

On Friday, it was well after midnight when Eric returned to his apartment. He'd thought Ashley's party would have ended, but even before he stepped out of the stairwell onto the second floor, he could hear the music and the sound of voices. Her door was open, people spilling out into the hallway. Two women were seated on the carpeting near his door, sipping drinks and deep in conversation. They barely noticed him. The man and woman at the end of the hallway were oblivious to everything, their bodies so close, they could have been Siamese twins.

He slipped into his apartment and tried to ignore the noise. His eyes were tired from too many hours spent poring over fine print and filling in figures, his body weary from a day of helping with the construction on the building. He took a quick shower, then began his usual meditation practice.

Only this night it didn't work.

A soft laugh from the opposite side of the wall brought him back to total awareness. He knew it was Ashley's laugh. Over the last few days, he'd heard it several times. She was a woman who laughed easily. Naturally.

Eyes closed, he tried to imagine what she was laughing at now. How she was dressed.

All three women in the hallway had been wearing jeans and fashionable tops. Ashley would look good in jeans. Tight-fitting jeans. And an equally tight-fitting top.

He felt a tightening in his own body and forced his thoughts in another direction.

The last thing he'd seen her wearing was a suit. A tailored, demure charcoal suit that hid more than showed off her figure. She'd had it on that morning. He'd been looking out his bedroom window and had spotted her dashing across the street to her car. Only a red scarf at the collar had given the outfit any color. That and the golden, taffy hue of her hair.

Once again she'd had it pulled back in a twist. He'd wondered then and he wondered now if she ever wore it down and how long it was. For some foolish reason he wanted to see her hair down. Feel it. Run his fingers through it.

Again his body began to respond.

He didn't like the ideas that kept popping into his head. Concentrating, he breathed deeply and slowly and tried to center himself.

He thought he was succeeding until someone turned up the volume of her stereo. A few minutes later it was once again down to a tolerable level, and he started over.

He did not feel truly relaxed when he went to bed, and as tired as he was, sleep did not come. Then, at two o'clock, the stereo once again blared forth.

This time no one turned it down, and finally Eric gave up. He pulled on a pair of black jeans and a black turtleneck, then ran his fingers through his hair, giving the thick, shaggy locks some semblance of order. At his door he slipped on his black running shoes.

He didn't need to knock on Ashley's door. It was still open, but the number of people at her party had greatly diminished. He paused in the doorway and looked around.

Actually, there were still several people in the small one-bedroom apartment—some seated, some standing, most in small groups. They were talking, drinking wine or beer, and nibbling on food.

To his left, in the dining area, the table was set buffet-style, with a variety of trays and bowls holding chips, dips, and snacks. And to his right was her stereo. He didn't see Ashley and was about to head for the stereo, when he heard her laugh. A moment later she came out of the kitchen, still laughing and holding a glass of wine.

Involuntarily, he caught his breath.

Her hair was in its usual twist, but his guesses at what she'd be wearing hadn't come anywhere near reality. Shimmering silk and lustrous leather, however, suited her.

No, his imagined outfits hadn't been anything like

what she was wearing, but his body was reacting the same as it had earlier.

She saw him, and her laughter turned to a welcoming smile. Wherever she'd been headed, she changed her mind and walked directly toward him.

He watched her near, noticing how her soft, smooth black leather pants flowed over slim hips and down curvaceous legs like a second skin. The iridescent teal color of her silk blouse changed with each step she took. One moment the material clung to her with tempting clarity, the next it billowed out, giving only a hint of what he'd seen. He'd never considered himself a breast man, yet it took a concerted effort for him to pull his gaze back to her eyes.

"You came," she said, surprising him by wrapping an arm around his neck, the gold bracelets on her wrist clinking musically. Before he could respond, she rose up on the toes of her stockinged feet and kissed his cheek, all the while holding her glass away so the wine wouldn't spill on them.

She wobbled a little, and he automatically put his hands on her waist, balancing her. She giggled, and he had a feeling she'd had one too many glasses of wine. That would explain her unexpected kiss. But it did not explain the urge he felt to turn his head and kiss her on the mouth.

To taste her.

To make love to her.

Those were crazy thoughts. He'd come to her apartment to get her to turn down her stereo. That was all. He needed to remember his mission.

"I was wondering if you could turn down the volume a little?" he asked.

Ashley wished she could disappear. Talk about making a fool of herself. Here she'd thought Eric had come to her party because he'd finished his work and wanted to see her. But no, he'd come over because her stereo was too loud.

And what did she do?

She greeted him like a long-lost friend. Kissed him. Acted like a drunken idiot.

All because she found him incredibly attractive and tantalizingly mysterious.

Well, she wasn't all that intoxicated, and no matter what his reason for coming, he was at her party. Settling back on her heels, she grinned. If she had her way, he was going to stay awhile.

"I'll be glad to turn the volume down," she promised. "But first, I want you to meet your neighbors."

Before he could object, she called out to those in the room. "Hey, everyone, this is Eric Newman. Our new neighbor. He's come to say hello."

She had put Eric in a position where he couldn't leave without being rude. As she'd expected, he nodded and smiled at the men and women who had stopped their conversations to turn and look at him.

"Come on," she said, pulling on his arm and leading him toward her couch. "You've got to meet each one personally. After all, you've been the talk of the party tonight."

"I have?"

"Oh, yes." And she'd listened to every word she

could hear. "You're quite the mystery man. No one seems to know anything about you."

"There is not much to know."

She doubted that.

Ashley introduced him to Liz Behmer, who considered herself the resident psychologist; to Andrew McGee and the group he was entertaining with his poetry; to the unmarried couple who lived down the hall; to the two men who lived in the apartment above her; and to the half-dozen men and women who worked for her or in other departments at Stedfeld's. "Virginia, my secretary, and Rod, one of the other directors from work, are in the kitchen," she added, motioning in that direction. "Charlie just went downstairs for some wine he wants us to try, and Dave Pacheco is in the bedroom with—"

She didn't finish. Charlie entered the apartment just then, carrying an unopened bottle of wine. "This you have got to try," he said, heading straight for them and smiling at Eric. "So you came after all."

"I thought perhaps I could get the music turned down a bit." Eric glanced toward her stereo, and Ashley knew her play for time hadn't changed his mind about staying. Still, she hoped she could keep him around, learn more about him—discover why he'd been on her mind since the last time she'd seen him.

"Dave's not finished with his dance," she explained. "As soon as he is, I'll turn it down."

Eric's eyebrows rose questioningly, but before he said anything, Charlie spoke up. "Heard something interesting today . . . about a ninja working for the police department."

Immediately, Eric looked at him. "From where did you hear that?"

"I've got a friend on the force, an old buddy who's gonna retire any day now. I told him I knew a real live ninja, and he said he'd heard rumors that a couple years ago there was a ninja working for them, that the guy was involved with some very secretive special project. Said, from what he heard, this guy always dressed in black."

Charlie's gaze slid from Eric's black turtleneck, down past his black jeans, to his black running shoes. Then he smiled. "Whaddaya think?"

Ashley knew what she thought. Charlie suspected the ninja was Eric.

Eric's expression never changed. Solemnly, he studied Charlie, then answered, "Those who practice the art of ninjutsu often dress in black. But your friend does not speak wisely. As a law-abiding citizen, I would be very concerned if I heard that a ninja was working for the police. I would ask myself what project was this man working on that was so secretive? And was not something like that against the law?"

"Those thoughts did cross my mind," Charlie admitted. "Also crossed my mind that it might be you. Would it be?"

"I am a teacher of martial arts. On occasion I have worked with police officers on methods of self-defense. To believe I do anything beyond that is to believe in rumors."

Ashley watched Eric the entire time he answered Charlie and marveled at how little she could tell from his expression or body language. He was a man in control of his emotions and his thinking . . . and he thought quickly. She admired the deft way he'd answered Charlie, in essence not answering him at all. She wished she could get some of her clients to be as straightforwardly evasive when talking to the press.

"How long have you lived in Ann Arbor?" Charlie asked, clearly still working on the idea.

"What has it been?" Eric smiled slightly. "About ten days now?"

Charlie frowned. "You've never lived in Ann Arbor before you moved here?"

"Never." Eric switched his gaze to Ashley. She had said nothing, yet he knew she'd been following every word of their conversation, coming to her own conclusions. In her blue eyes he saw the same confusion that was reflected in Charlie's. Neither knew what to make of his answers, which was fine.

He looked back at Charlie. "I've lived in Tokyo, Kyoto, New York City, and Detroit. While growing up, I spent six months of the year in the States and six months in Japan. Up until now, I have considered myself somewhat of a nomad."

"But now you're settling down?" Ashley asked.

Again he glanced her way. "If I can get enough students to come to my dojo, I will. Perhaps I should hire you to do some publicity for me."

She smiled. "Perhaps."

He loved her smile. And her mouth, her lips so full and tempting. He should have kissed her earlier. No, he should never have come. Being around her was like drinking sake. He had to be careful—limit himself— or he would forget everything and lose control.

"I see you brought the wine," a new voice said, and Eric looked in that direction. A stocky middle-aged man was walking toward them.

"This is Rod . . . Rod Bowman," Ashley said. "He's one of the other directors at Stedfeld's and has been like a father to me, helped me when I was a lowly editor and taught me the ropes about public relations."

She introduced him, and Eric shook his hand. "Newman," Rod repeated, studying his face. "My daughter used to talk about an Eric Newman when she was going to the University of Michigan. By any chance would that be you?"

"If she was there two years ago and taking classes in Japanese culture, it was," Eric said. "I was a guest instructor."

"She was there, and she majored in languages." Rod laughed. "What a small world. My daughter used to talk about you all the time. Said you were the best teacher she'd ever had, that listening to you, she could finally understand what the others had been saying."

Eric bowed. "I am pleased that I was able to assist her with her learning."

He might be pleased, Ashley thought, but she was curious. When Charlie spoke up, she knew he'd been wondering the same thing.

"I thought you said you'd never lived in Ann Arbor before."

Eric looked at Charlie, then at her. "I spoke the truth. When I was giving those seminars, I was commuting from Detroit."

A moot point, Ashley decided. Commuting or not, he'd been in the area, and that left open the question of whether he'd been the ninja working for the police.

Her mystery man was becoming all the more mysterious.

"If it means anything," Rod went on, "my daughter had a king-sized crush on you. I once overheard her telling a friend that you were the best-looking teacher she'd ever had."

Ashley wouldn't argue, though she wouldn't really call Eric handsome, not in the classic definition. His dark hair had a shaggy appearance, falling low on his forehead, covering the tops of his ears, and reaching to his collar. And with his almond-shaped eyes and narrow nose, "unique" better described him. Distinctive.

Actually, what attracted her more than his looks was the sense of power he projected, the feeling of controlled energy. Even as he stood beside her, seemingly relaxed, she knew he was alert to everything going on around him. Alert and ready.

"Charlie . . . ?" a timid voice called from the kitchen.

"That's Virginia, my secretary," Ashley told Eric. "She's new."

"She's also upset about June," Charlie said, shaking his head. "What she needs is a dose of self-confidence." He glanced at the bottle in his hand. "Maybe a little of this will help."

As Charlie walked away, Rod chuckled. "Speaking of self-confidence, have you noticed old Jimbo didn't show up tonight?"

"Did you really think he would?" Ashley laughed, then turned to Eric to explain. "Jim Stanton is the other director where I work. He's upset because I want to transfer to Chicago."

"And so does he," Rod said.

Ashley doubted that Eric understood, so she went on. "Stedfeld's main office is in Chicago, but there are branch offices in more than twenty cities in five states. Whenever there's an opening at a branch or at the main office, we get a notice of it and have an opportunity to apply. There are rarely any good ones for Chicago—once people get there, they seem to stay—but just last Monday we got the notice of a director's position opening up."

"Which Jim wants," Rod said.

"And so do I. In fact, I've always wanted to work in Chicago. But when I graduated from college, the only job opening anywhere in Stedfeld's was here. Which really hasn't been all bad. I've been getting promotions fairly regularly, and—"

Rod interrupted her, chuckling. "Regularly, she says. This woman is a dynamo. I've never seen anyone catch on as quickly as she does. Usually, a new hire starts out writing press releases and after five years develops enough expertise to be part of client strategy sessions. This gal was there within one year. Within three she was managing clients. And whereas it usually takes a person ten or more years to become a director, she'd done it in five."

"Why waste time?" Ashley said. She grinned at Eric and wondered what he thought of women with goals and lots of drive. Most men, she'd discovered, were intimidated by her.

Eric didn't look intimidated. In fact, she liked the

way he was looking at her, deep into her eyes, into her soul. She hoped he couldn't tell how much he fascinated her.

"Now's your chance," Rod said, jarring her back to what they were discussing, "to be a big shot in the firm, have prestigious, important accounts, and live in a condo that overlooks Lake Michigan."

"*If*," she said, "I can convince the committee by January that I'm the best for the job."

"Ah, the committee you mentioned," Eric said, nodding and smiling. "The one you would like to hypnotize."

"Right. I—"

"Hey, Rod, could you come here a minute?" Charlie called from the kitchen.

"Sounds like he's having problems," Rod said. "Will you two please excuse me? My turn to hold a hand, I think." He took a step, then stopped and looked back at Eric. "If you ever meet my daughter, don't tell her what I told you she said about you. She'd kill me."

"Your words are forgotten," Eric assured him.

Suddenly, from the bedroom, a woman crudely yelled, "Take it all off!"

Rod grinned at Ashley. "Sounds like the party's getting wild in there."

"I hate to think what's going on." Ashley glanced toward her bedroom. The door was open a crack, and through it she got a glimpse of a man's bare, hairy leg. "That's Dave Pacheco," she told Eric. "He lives upstairs, and he's a male stripper. June Halder is one of Jim's assistants, and I was hoping she wouldn't come tonight. I don't think this woman was hired for her brains. In fact, to give you an idea, her nickname around the office is 'the blond bombshell.' "

"And this Dave is stripping for her?" Eric asked, staring at the bedroom door.

"Supposedly, he's just giving her and a couple other women a demonstration of his act. I told him I didn't want him taking off *all* of his clothes." She glanced up at Eric. "But I'm not going to check if he's following orders."

"No curiosity?"

"Hey, I had an older brother. I know what men look like."

"Just from having an older brother?"

She knew he was baiting her, but she wasn't about to give him any satisfaction. "I did peek in a few *Playgirls.*"

The door to her bedroom opened. A tall blond man in his early twenties rushed out, wearing nothing more than a pair of navy skivvies and carrying his shirt, jeans, and shoes. Two women followed him, laughing.

Ashley could tell Dave was upset. Nervously checking back over his shoulder, he stopped in front of her. "That woman is crazy," he gasped. "I've never come across one that aggressive."

"I warned you," she said, laughing.

He began to pull on his jeans, all the while keeping an eye on the bedroom door. Another woman stepped out of the bedroom, straightening her sweater, then running a hand through her shoulder-length blond hair. Dave tensed, missing his pant leg and hopping about on one leg. The woman stopped, her gaze going first to Dave, then to Ashley, then to Eric.

Dave got both legs into his jeans and pulled up the zipper. He didn't bother to button them. "I'm leaving," he said to Ashley. "And don't you dare tell that woman what apartment I'm in."

"Aren't you the one who's always telling me that in your business it pays to advertise?" Ashley laughed as Dave escaped out of the apartment; then she faced Eric. "For months he's been coming on to me. A little of his own medicine serves him right."

Eric nodded. "One learns best from experience."

What kind of experiences had he had? she wondered. And what would it be like to be loved by a man like him?

Just the thought made her giddy. She started to take a sip from her wineglass, then realized it was empty. It was just as well, she decided. If she was thinking of making love with a man, she'd had too much to drink.

Charlie walked back out of the kitchen just then, his usual smile gone. "Can you come?" he asked, nodding back toward the kitchen. "It's your secretary. She's been crying for the last five minutes. I can't get her to stop, and neither can Rod. You've got to talk to her."

"What's the problem?"

"She's sure you're upset because she brought June tonight. She thinks you're going to fire her."

"Fire her?" Ashley glanced at Eric. "Give me a minute?"

"I really should go."

He was probably right, but she didn't want him to go. Not yet. "Please stay. Just a little while longer." She gave him what she hoped was a plaintive look. "We still haven't had a chance to talk."

He hesitated, then nodded.

"I'll get you something to drink while I'm in there," she said. "What would you like? Some of Charlie's wine? A beer? Soft drink?"

"I think I'd prefer a beer."

"One beer coming up." She started for the kitchen, then paused. "You will be here when I get back, won't you?"

"I will be here," Eric promised, but as he watched Ashley go through the doorway, he wondered if that was wise. The more time he spent with her, the more he liked her. Next thing he knew, he'd be staying until everyone else had left her party.

And then who knew what might happen.

No, what he needed to do was what he'd come to do. Turn down the volume of her stereo. Then he should get out, head for his own bed. Maybe he wouldn't get a lot of sleep, but come morning he'd be a lot happier with himself.

He had the volume down to a reasonable level when the blond woman from the bedroom came up behind him. Close behind him. "Hi," she purred. "My name's June. And what's yours?"

Slowly, he rose to his feet and faced her. "My name is Eric."

She stepped closer, crowding him. With the stereo on one side, and walls behind him and to the other side, there was nowhere for him to go.

"Well, Eric, it's nice to meet you." She edged even closer. "You a friend of Ashley's?"

"Neighbor." He could escape if he had to, but he didn't want to make a scene. This was a situation that called for a little talk. A little fast talk.

He didn't talk fast enough. Before he even thought of something to say, a pair of humongous breasts were pressed against his chest. "Wanna be neighborly?" June murmured.

He sensed her hand going for his crotch and blocked it. She looked surprised. "Whatsa matter with all you men? Don't you know how to party?"

"Party's over," Ashley announced loudly, coming up behind June, and Eric smiled in relief. Never before had he been rescued by a woman. He welcomed it now.

Almost immediately, throughout the room, people began to move toward the door. June, however, didn't budge an inch. Seductively, she smiled up at Eric. "Let's party at your place."

"He's mine, June," Ashley said quietly, just barely loud enough for the woman to hear. "Virginia's waiting for you. She's ready to go home."

"It's still early," June insisted, and looked back at Eric. She puckered her lips, and he melded into the wall.

"*This* party's over," Ashley repeated firmly.

Disgruntled, June glanced at her. "He's really yours?"

"Yes."

Sighing with frustration, she pushed herself away, and Eric took in a deep breath. The air around him reeked of alcohol and cigarette smoke. He could understand the stripper's dash out of the bedroom, and why the man had asked Ashley not to reveal his apartment number. Eric knew he had no intention of letting June know he lived right next door.

It was better to let her think what Ashley had said was true. Casually, he positioned himself next to Ashley and draped an arm around her shoulders. He felt her tense, then she glanced up and smiled, hooking an arm around his waist, confirming the union.

"You want me to hang around?" Charlie asked, coming up beside Ashley. "Give you a hand cleaning up or anything?"

"We can take care of it," Eric said.

Charlie glanced at him, then at Ashley, nodded, and smiled. He left with Rod.

Soon only June and Virginia remained, but getting June to leave wasn't as easy as Eric had hoped. First the woman couldn't find her purse. Virginia finally remembered June hadn't brought one. Next she had to get a drink of water. Then she had to go to the bathroom. Her excuses having run out, she stood at the door, ignoring Virginia's pleas to hurry. Over and over she gushed to Ashley about the wonderful time she'd had. Eric noticed he was the one she was looking at.

At last, Virginia dragged June down the hallway.

Slowly, Ashley closed the door.

THREE

Eric glanced around the now-empty room. "Your friends left a mess. But it will clean up quickly."

Ashley shook her head. "Let's just leave it. All I really need to do is get the food in the fridge before I head for bed."

Suddenly unsure if that might sound as though she were suggesting he join her in bed, especially after what she'd said to June, she hurried to explain. "I mean, I'll get the food and go to bed after you've left. Not that you have to leave right away. I just—"

She stopped, afraid she was really going to put her foot in her mouth if she kept talking. He smiled. "I think I had better stay for a few minutes. I would not put it past that woman to wait out there for me."

"It would be like her," Ashley admitted, and stepped away from the door. He was staying. Here in her apartment. For a while there would be just the two of them. Alone. Together.

Now all she had to do was get her insides to stop quivering and her heart to stop beating faster than a hummingbird's wings. Her earlier idea that spending some time with Eric would lessen the attraction hadn't worked. Not one bit.

"Is your June always like that?" he asked.

Ashley glanced at him. "From what I've heard, she is. But she's not mine. June works for Jim. I never really see her. Virginia is my secretary. I just got her this week."

Needing more room between them, Ashley walked over to her stereo. The music playing was definitely romantic. She stopped the tape and crouched down, looking through her selection of cassettes.

"Virginia is nice," Eric said, his words spoken softly and amazingly close.

So close, Ashley started and dropped the tape in her hand. He'd come up beside her, and she hadn't even heard him. Her nerves already tensed, she held her breath and waited, unsure of what to expect next.

Squatting beside her, he picked up the tape she'd dropped and handed it to her. Then he glanced over her selection. "It has been a while since I have listened to this kind of music. KISS?"

She swallowed hard, her gaze dropping to his mouth. Barely breathing, she licked her lips.

"Do you like them?" he asked, looking at her.

Her pulse rate went wild. "Kisses?"

"No, the group." He pointed to the one and only tape she had by KISS.

"They're okay," she mumbled, feeling like an idiot.

She knew she was blushing, and her voice was shaky. If he noticed, he said nothing. Continuing to look at her tapes, he picked out another. "How about this one?"

"U2? Yeah, they're great. I'll put it on." She took the cassette and quickly started it, keeping the volume low.

They both stood. "Thank you for rescuing me earlier," he said. "I am sorry it meant ending your party."

"It was time for it to end. As for June . . ." Ashley hesitated. "I wasn't really sure what to do, at first."

She still remembered how she'd felt when she'd walked out of the kitchen and seen June pressing herself against Eric. She'd wanted to grab the woman by the hair and pull her off. And that wasn't like her. She was a person who avoided fights. Especially fights over a man. Her rule was not to get emotionally involved with anyone. Not until she reached her goal and fulfilled her promise.

Tonight, though, she'd been ready to fight for Eric, and she couldn't believe what she'd actually said. "I hope you don't mind my saying you belonged to me. It just popped into my head."

Slowly, his gaze moved from her face, down over the front of her silk blouse, to her leather pants. When he met her eyes again, just a hint of a smile touched his lips. "I cannot think of anyone I would rather belong to."

What had been a flutter in her stomach became a complete invasion of butterflies. "Oh, come now," she nearly pleaded. "I'm sure you have a girlfriend somewhere. Maybe back in Japan?"

He shook his head. "No girlfriend, here or there. And what about you? A boyfriend somewhere?"

Once again, she felt the mesmerizing power of his gaze. She couldn't have lied if she'd wanted to. "There's no one," she whispered.

Suddenly afraid of the emotions spiraling through her, she hurried on. "What I mean is, I don't have time for romance. I'm going to Chicago. I—"

She fell silent, and he said nothing. The only sounds in the room were the pulsating beat of the music coming from the stereo and their breathing. His was as shallow as hers.

The look in his eyes was hypnotic.

Slowly, tentatively, he reached out and touched the side of her face. Finally, he spoke. "You are very pretty, Ashley-san."

And he was sexy and exciting, and she couldn't stop herself. She matched his touch, letting her fingers graze the side of his chin. She could barely feel any stubble. What she felt was cool skin, the twitch of a cheek muscle, and the power of his gaze. It left her breathless. "What you are is intriguing."

He smiled and caught her hand in his. "It is you who are intriguing. A spark of fire. A brisk wind. The essence of a woman."

"Really?" She searched for words to describe him. A maelstrom. An emotional tornado. Virility.

"What is it you are looking for, Ashley-san?" he asked quietly.

What she wanted, she thought, was a way to understand this fascination, this desire to touch and be near him. A way to vanquish him from her thoughts and dreams, to stop her heart from beating so wildly every time he smiled at her. She wanted to be over this craziness, to regain control of her thoughts and emotions. It was too frightening.

Abruptly, she pulled her hand free from his and stepped back. "I'm looking for the usual. Happiness. Money. And . . ."—she knew she had to change the subject. It was getting too serious—"maybe some of Charlie's wine."

She edged even farther back. "You want some too?"

He shook his head. "No, thank you."

"Whatever."

She turned away and headed for the kitchen, and Eric's gaze was drawn to the sway of her hips, the leather hugging her there, smoothly delineating every enticing curve. It seemed that everything about Ashley turned him on—the way she talked and smiled, her walk, her sexy backside.

At her breakfast counter she paused and glanced back. "I forgot. It was a beer you wanted, wasn't it?"

"Do not bother." He didn't need a beer. What he needed was a cold shower. The physical attraction between them had become a viable force, stirring a need in him that had been dormant for months and was making his jeans uncomfortably tight.

When they were touching, and even before then, he'd noticed similar signs of arousal in her—her flushed cheeks, the darkening of her blue eyes, and the hardened nubs of her nipples pressing against her silk blouse. It was obvious Ashley was fighting her feelings, just as he should be fighting his. They were opposites. They came from different worlds.

From the kitchen he heard the clink of a glass and her bracelets and took a deep breath. Yes, intriguing described her, not him. He didn't understand her . . . or his reaction to her. He should leave. Wipe her out of his mind.

"I must be going now," he called, and started for the door to the hallway.

"I poured a beer for you," she said, stepping back into the living room, a wineglass in one hand, a tall plastic cup in the other. "It's fresh from the keg. You can take it with you, if you'd like."

"I must go," he repeated, but looking at her, he felt his resolve falter. "It is late."

"Very late," she agreed, starting toward him.

He didn't move. He wasn't one to run from danger, not even emotional danger. To run would answer nothing. He needed to stay, face these confusing feelings, and understand them.

With determination he made up his mind. What he would do was control the attraction he felt for Ashley. Control and ignore it.

He met her halfway. "Perhaps I will have that beer. Do you have these parties often?"

"Oh, no. This is only the second one I've had in the three years I've lived here. Parties are for major accomplishments."

He took the cup from her hand, their fingers brushing, and sparks of awareness coursed through his body. From the way her eyes grew wider, he knew she'd felt it too. He stepped back, keeping a distance between them, and silently laughed at himself. So much for control.

She seemed to be better at it. "When I got my first client," she said, glancing around the room, "I got a keg of beer, and we partied all night. Now that I'm director of Public Relations, it's beer and wine." She lifted her wineglass. "If . . . No, *when* I get that transfer to Chicago, it will be champagne."

"Here's to champagne," he said, lifting his beer.

"To champagne."

He watched her take a long sip of her wine, then he drank from his cup. The beer was cool and bubbly, the taste sharp. Lowering her glass, she ran the tip of her tongue over her lips, and he suppressed a groan. He wanted to run *his* tongue over those lips, taste her, discover if her mouth was firm and cool or soft and warm.

She caught him staring, and he jerked his gaze away. His mind was not behaving as it should, as it had been trained. Nor was his body.

He forced himself to concentrate on what she'd been saying. "This transfer is between you and that other man?"

"Jim? Yes. And probably a half-dozen other directors from other branches. These next few months are going to be the telling ones. I've got to impress the hell out of the screening committee. Work my buns off."

"Now that sounds interesting." He couldn't stop himself from glancing down at her leather pants. Yes, she had very nice buns.

She noticed the direction of his gaze and frowned.

"You probably don't think I'm serious about this, but I am. I don't have time for men or romance or anything but my work."

"Ah, but I do understand." He'd been making sacrifices for his work for years. Would be for years to come. "When you want something very much, you have to make choices. Sometimes those choices mean putting pleasures aside."

Now, if he could just convince his body of that.

"Exactly," she said enthusiastically. "I mean, it's not that I'm not attracted to a man once in a while. . . ." She paused, her gaze locked on his face. Then she shook her head and looked away. "But not right now. Now, I just can't let it happen."

"Not and reach your goal, is that it?"

"Yes." She turned away, walking toward the buffet table. "For instance," she said, and began picking at the food that was still out. "If I were to get involved with a man right now, he would want to be with me, would be jealous of all the time I spend at the office, and would be upset by all the work I bring home. Soon we'd be arguing. It would be a mess."

"A total mess," he agreed. "Just like the mess that would happen if I got involved with a woman who did not understand what I am looking for in life. There would be too many complications. So, the best thing to do is avoid the situation."

Ashley stared at him. He did understand. So why, she wondered, did she feel so confused and unnerved? So disappointed with his answer.

She nibbled on a carrot stick, popped a few potato

chips into her mouth, then took another sip of wine. Charlie was right. It was a good wine. Mellow.

Potent.

She could feel a buzz in her head. She could also sense Eric's gaze on her, and she grabbed another chip. She had no idea why she was eating, or drinking. Her stomach was in knots, so food was the last thing she wanted, and alcohol—sweet, inhibition-dulling alcohol—was the last thing she needed.

No, Eric Newman was the last thing she needed. Yet she wanted to know him better. Wanted a chance to discover whatever it was that made him so attractive to her. Slowly, she started back toward him. "What are you looking for in life, Mr. Eric Newman?"

"Enlightenment."

"Enlightenment?" A need for love, she could understand, probably more than most. Or a desire for financial success. Or for fame. Enlightenment, however, was a philosophical goal. It had no substance, no body.

Step by step she drew closer to him. "And how do you know when you've found enlightenment?"

His chuckle was throaty, his look wary, as she neared. "I suppose, if you are enlightened, you know."

"I guess that's reasonable." She laughed louder than necessary and knew she was getting drunk. She had to be. Otherwise, she wouldn't be flirting with danger. She stopped directly in front of him. "What's it like to be a ninja warrior?"

"Nothing like you see on television or in the movies."

"Are you the ninja who's working with the police?"

Teasingly, she edged closer. "Are you making the world a better place for poor helpless damsels like me?"

He cleared his throat and took in a quick breath. "And are you a helpless damsel?"

"Of course." She knew she was bothering him, and it only seemed fair. For the last few nights thoughts about him had been bothering her. "Will you save me?"

"From what?"

"From you." She laid the palm of a hand against his chest and felt the heat of his body, the thud of his heart. She'd meant to unnerve him a little, but she was the one who was shaken.

Jerking her hand back, she turned and took a step away. "Why have you come to Ann Arbor?"

"It is a good city, not too big, not too small. From my earlier connection with the college, I know people, already have a few students who will come to my dojo. Why is going to Chicago so important to you?"

She was glad he'd asked. She needed the reminder. "Because, since I was ten, I've had that as my goal. It's a promise I made."

"And if you don't make it?"

She wouldn't allow herself to consider that possibility. "I will make it," she insisted.

"Then you'd better enjoy those pants while you can." Grinning, he glanced down at her hips.

She also looked down, running a hand over the smooth leather that covered her thigh. "I don't understand," she said, frowning at him.

"Well, if you are going to work your buns off,

those pants are not going to fit as well as they do now." His gaze switched from her hips to her face, and for a moment she saw the raw need in his eyes. Then he breathed deeply and set his near-empty cup on an end table. "I will go now."

Yes, go, she said silently. *Get out of my life, out of my dreams.*

The problem was, sending him on his way wasn't going to stop what she was feeling, wasn't going to satisfy her curiosity.

If you have a problem, face it. That was what her father always used to tell her brother when he was in trouble. Well, it was time for her to face her problem, deal with it.

"You know," she said softly, "you haven't congratulated me on my promotion to director."

"I am sorry." He bowed. "I am very pleased for you, Ashley-san."

Grinning seductively, she placed her glass on the end table beside his. "Most of the men tonight gave me a kiss."

He tensed. "And do you really think that is a wise idea?"

"Afraid?"

She was, yet she knew from past experience that the anticipation of a kiss was always more exhilarating than the actual experience.

"A little fear can often keep a man from making a mistake."

"Or can keep him wondering." Wrapping her arms around his neck, she rose up on her toes. "I suppose I'm no different than June."

"Oh, you are nothing like June," he said hoarsely, but he didn't touch her, didn't give her any encouragement.

"It's just that I find you so intriguing."

"And I find you equally intriguing. But we are going to resist that feeling, is that not so?" Nevertheless, he reached behind her head and began removing the bobby pins holding her hair.

"Resist," she said huskily, watching the way he worked his mouth as he concentrated on his task.

"Do you always wear your hair up?" he asked, combing his fingers through its thickness until it all fell loosely to her shoulders.

"In business, a woman looks more sophisticated with her hair up."

"Sophisticated," he repeated. His fingers followed the flow of her hair down over her shoulders to her back. "It makes me think of taffy. Is the color natural?"

"Yes." And so was the feel of his hands on her body. Natural . . . and right.

And exciting.

She moaned, melting against him.

He kissed her then, his mouth capturing her lips with a masterful force. He kissed her firmly, passionately, and her fingers tightened on his shoulders.

She'd been wrong. Anticipation had not prepared her for this moment. Disappointment was not what she felt. Not with this kiss. Not with this man.

The feel of his lips on hers was all she'd dreamed of and more. He was strong yet gentle. Possessive yet giving. Her hands slid over his shoulders, up his neck to his hair. "Yes," she sighed against his mouth. "Oh, yes."

Eric felt her nails play against his scalp, tingly sensations skittering down his spine. Her bracelets jingled near his ear, and the music of a thousand centuries played through his body, a song of need and desire. Infatuation and lust. She opened her mouth to him, and he invaded, craving all she offered and more.

She tasted good. Felt good. He wanted to absorb and become a part of her, and as his hands slid down her silky smooth blouse to the soft leather covering her bottom, a shudder ran the length of him. Never had he felt so out of control.

Ashley could only cling to him, all reason long gone. She'd wanted a kiss. She'd thought it would cure her of the crazy dreams she'd been having, of the restless need he'd aroused. Now, she knew she'd merely opened Pandora's box. He was the darkness of mystery and the light of clarity. Temptation. Danger.

Eric Newman was everything she had so carefully avoided for so many years, a man she wouldn't be able to kiss and forget.

With his hands he stroked and caressed her, all the while murmuring words against her lips, against her cheek, into her ear. Foreign words that she didn't understand, no more than she understood what she was feeling. Nothing made any sense, not anymore. Then again, it all made perfect sense.

Her own hands moved over his back, the texture of his turtleneck smooth, the body beneath it as taut as a coiled spring. Somewhere deep in the fog of her mind she heard him groan, then she felt him pulling away. For a moment she held fast, breathing him in, absorbing every marvelous, mysterious sensation of him. Then she gave in to reality and pushed herself back, as off balance physically as she felt mentally.

He caught her hand, steadying her. In his eyes she saw the passion and need. "How far do you want this to go?" he asked.

How far? It had gone too far already . . . and not far enough. She was even more confused than before. Frustrated. "We've got to stop," she said, though her body begged the opposite. "I—"

She couldn't finish. Words wouldn't explain. Yet he seemed to understand. "I think I'd better leave."

She didn't object. Entwining her fingers with his, she stepped backward. Silently, steadily, she backed to her front door, her gaze never leaving his face, her breathing shallow, their locked hands uniting them.

She was still holding his hand when she opened the door. Eric wondered if they would spend the rest of the night standing in the hallway that way, then she released her hold, her arm dropping to her side. "Good luck with your martial-arts school."

"Thank you." He hesitated before leaving. The second she'd let go of his hand, he'd felt a sense of loss. How could he just walk away?

How could he not?

Taking a deep, cleansing breath, he edged out of her apartment. "Good luck on getting your transfer."

"Thanks." She managed a smile. "See you around."

She closed the door quickly. In the hallway he stood staring at the peephole, his thoughts a chaotic mess. Years of disciplined training struggled against raw emotions. He knew how to evade the stroke of a sword's blade, the thrust of a knife, or the jab of a cane, but a woman's kiss—this woman's kiss—was more lethal.

FOUR

Ashley could hear the Canadian geese flying overhead, honking and calling to each other. And she could see her brother in the distance, standing on the opposite side of the field, his shoulders so broad and his blond hair blowing in the wind, blowing like the tall grass that separated them. "I'm depending on you," he called to her.

"I'll do it," she promised.

Glancing around, she saw her parents standing off to the side, her father looking so proud, her mother smiling. "I'll do it," she repeated to them, but they didn't seem to hear.

They were looking at Jack.

"I got a promotion," she shouted to Jack. Only now the field seemed wider, the grass taller, making it harder to see him.

She hoped he could hear. "I've applied for a job in Chicago. It's just what you always wanted."

Desperate to close the distance between them, she began to run. The grass was thick and trapped her feet, tangling around them.

"Jack!" she screamed.

It was the sound of her cry that woke her . . . and a pain in her head. Sitting up with a jolt, she pinched her temples with her fingertips and stared at the white walls of her bedroom. A numb, empty sensation replaced the desperation that had filled her.

It had been a dream.

For a moment she could do no more than sit there, massaging her temples and staring at the wall, reliving the scene that had seemed so real. She could feel her top sheet wrapped around her feet, twisted and binding. And from outside her window she could hear the honking of geese flying south for the winter.

A dream. She sighed and lay back down.

She hadn't dreamed about Jack for quite a while. The feelings afterward were the same though—a sense of emptiness and confusion, pangs of guilt. In a way she should have expected this one. They always seemed to come after she made it a step closer to her goal . . . their goal.

Slowly, the memory of the dream faded from her thoughts, the pain in her head and the fuzzy, cottony taste in her mouth becoming her reality. What she had was a hangover.

Idiot! she chastised herself. She never should have drunk so much wine.

Never should have kissed Eric Newman.

And to think, she was the one who had begged him to kiss her. Practically forced him to.

"Idiot!" she repeated aloud, then wished she hadn't. Once again a sledgehammer hit her brain.

Deciding she had to do something about her headache, she staggered through the mess in the living room to the kitchen. The smell of stale beer and old cigarette smoke turned her stomach, and when she looked at the dirty glasses and dishes stacked in the sink, she groaned.

In the cupboard by the sink she found her bottle of aspirins. She swallowed two, along with a lot of water. Climbing onto a stool at the breakfast bar and bracing her elbows on the countertop, she cradled her head between her palms and tried to remember just exactly what had happened the night before.

Everything had been fine until June talked Dave into doing his strip routine. That was when the stereo had been turned up, which had brought Eric to her door. From that moment on, Ashley knew, she'd started making mistakes. First greeting him with a kiss, then not letting him leave.

Why, oh why, hadn't she just turned down her stereo, apologized, and let him go back to his apartment? Why had she kept him there, parading him about like a prize possession? Why had she told June he was hers?

Most of all, why had she asked for that kiss?

What a simpleton she'd been to think Eric Newman's kiss would be like other men's, to think that one kiss would wipe him from her thoughts, would eliminate the fascination.

No way. One kiss had merely made her want more . . . and more. The way she'd acted, it was a miracle she hadn't woken with him lying beside her.

A knock at the door made her jump, then groan.

"You up?" Charlie yelled from the hallway.

"I'm up," she mumbled, and wished he'd go away.

He didn't, and finally she gave in and went to the door. He took one look at her and laughed. "So how you feeling, sunshine? Can't say you look your best."

"Go away."

Again he laughed, glancing at her hair, which hung in a tangle around her face, then at her knee-length cotton nightshirt. Next he looked back toward her bedroom. "Our friend still here?"

"What friend?" she asked innocently.

"Your neighbor. Looked like you two were getting pretty chummy at the end there."

"That was all for June's sake. Eric left as soon as we were sure the coast was clear."

"Too bad." Charlie worked his way into her apartment. "Doesn't look like you did much cleaning up last night."

"Charlie, go away." The last thing she needed was his jovial chatter.

"Come on, I'll fix you something for that head," he promised, and guided her back to her kitchen.

Actually, he had to go down to his apartment to find the ingredients he needed, but after a half hour he had a mixture for her to drink. "Bottoms up," he encouraged.

She sniffed the concoction and wrinkled her nose. "What's in this?"

"Wonderful medicine." He helped her lift the glass to her mouth. "Drink up. I guarantee you'll feel better in no time."

She drank, then sat on her barstool and watched as Charlie picked up the mess in her living room, stacked the dirty dishes in her dishwasher, and brought her apartment back to a semblance of order. And within a half hour she did begin to feel human again.

Giving the counter a final swipe, he smiled at her. "Back with the living?"

"Sort of."

"So what do you think?"

"That I'm not going to have that much to drink again."

"No, I mean about our ninja friend. Is he the one my friend was talking about? Is he working with the police?"

"Could be," she decided. "But he's probably right. The less said, the better."

"My lips are sealed." Charlie made a gesture of locking his lips, then patted her hand. "He'd be good for you."

"Charlie . . ." Ashley stopped, knowing nothing she said would make any difference. He'd made up his mind. Smiling, she finished. "Thanks for the help."

"Any time." He grinned and headed for her door. "Great party. Good way to get to know people."

Perhaps, but she really wasn't sure if getting to know people was such a good idea. Not when she found one so irresistible. This was not the time to be making new friends. Maybe that's why she'd had the dream. It was her subconscious warning her that what she needed to do was concentrate on her job.

The best thing for her, she decided, was not to get to know, but to avoid any and all contact with, her new neighbor.

Over the next few days Ashley discovered being able to hear through the walls was an advantage. She could tell when Eric was in his apartment and when he was gone. All she had to do was time her comings and goings so they didn't run into each other.

Not that she was around her own apartment that much. Ever since her promotion to the position of director, she'd been spending more time at the office. Which was fine with her. She loved the work and was sure the extra hours were bringing her closer to her goal. One day soon she would be working in Chicago.

Then she would have fulfilled her promise to Jack and her promise to her father.

Exactly one week after her party Ashley worked unusually late. On the way home she stopped at the twenty-four-hour supermarket near the apartment building. She needed laundry soap, a few personal items, and some food. Most of the time she grabbed a hamburger at a fast-food restaurant or had a pizza delivered, but occasionally she liked to pop a frozen dinner into the microwave. She blamed those few weak moments on a residual memory of her mother nagging her and her brother to eat their vegetables.

A memory left over from when her mother would nag, would even acknowledge her existence.

Once in the market Ashley didn't waste time, and she was glad the store was nearly empty. As she sped up and down the aisles, she grabbed the items she needed, adding a few things that caught her eye and looked easy to prepare. Within a short time she had two boxes of breakfast bars, a multitude of frozen dinners, a few cans of soup, several boxes of frozen deep-fried, southern-style chicken, and two packages of frozen minipizzas. The only items she had left to find were peanut butter, bread, and a quart of milk.

She was hitting a good clip when she swung her cart around the end of the cereal aisle, heading for the peanut butter. As deserted as the store was, she didn't expect to meet up with anyone. Certainly not with someone *right* in her way.

But she did.

The moment she saw the cart, she reacted. With a tug and a jerk to the right, she pulled her cart out of the way. She immediately realized her error.

Carts in motion—especially in fast motion—had minds of their own. The front of hers headed straight for a stack of spaghetti-sauce jars. Though she tried to stop it, she just didn't have the leverage. Not for a cart as heavy as hers had become. Not going the speed she'd been going.

Then the flash of a hand and a blur of black stopped her wayward cart with a jarring shudder. Just like that, the crisis was over. The jars were safe.

Dazed, Ashley looked at the man who had saved her from having to explain to the store manager how

she'd "just accidentally" wiped out a shelf full of spa-
ghetti sauce. She wasn't surprised her good Samaritan
was Eric. Somehow she'd known it would be.

He was dressed in black—a black sweatshirt, black
sweats, and black running shoes—and he looked as
sexy and mysterious as she remembered. Her insides
did a flip, and her already accelerated heart began to
beat even faster. "Thank you," she said, the words
shaky.

He bowed slightly.

"You did it so . . ." She didn't know how to explain.
Quickly. Smoothly. Efficiently. "What do you do, go
around stopping shopping carts from ramming into
shelves every day?"

He smiled. "Every day I practice stopping objects
from moving in directions I do not want them to go.
A cart is easier to control than most things I stop."

His gaze traveled down over her tailored navy
pinstriped suit to her two-inch navy heels. "You look
nice. Very businesslike. Very sophisticated, as usual."

"I just came from work."

"It is late."

"I worked late." She knew her answer sounded
dumb. The problem was, she just couldn't seem to
think straight.

His gaze moved to her hair, and she remembered
how he'd said he liked it down. How he'd taken it
down only a week ago. Pin by pin, he'd set it free,
then run his fingers through it.

Her scalp tingled with the memory, and she nervously patted the side of her head, making certain her
hair was still pulled back in a twist. He wasn't doing

anything but looking at her, and she felt as though she were falling apart.

"You're looking . . . good," she managed, needing something to say and certain that telling a man he looked sexy as all get-out wasn't wise. Not when that man kissed as Eric did. Or when just standing near him could make her so uneasy. "How's the dojo coming along?"

He nodded. "Work on it is going well. Most of it is completed. I should be able to open soon."

"That's good." She licked her lips and wished she could think of something else to say, something that didn't sound totally inane.

"Will you come?" he asked.

"Come?"

"To my dojo. Will you take lessons? Learn self-defense?"

"Oh, I don't think so."

"I am going to have a special class for those who simply want to learn how to protect and defend themselves from danger. Once it has started, you are welcome to check it out."

"Maybe . . . sometime."

He was watching her intently, increasing her unease. To avoid his gaze, she looked down at the contents of her cart.

Eric looked too. "That is what you eat?"

The disdain in his voice surprised her, and she glanced back up. "Sure."

"All you have is junk food."

She picked up the closest item. "This is chicken. It's good for you."

"Not when it is breaded and fried in grease." He reached with both hands for the box. "May I?"

She gave it to him, and Eric knew he could have taken it without touching her. Could have, but he didn't. Instead, he let his fingers graze hers. Seeing her eyes widen slightly, he knew her nerves were as tightly strung as his.

She said nothing as he read over the list of ingredients on the label. Purposefully, he lingered over each item, listening to the ragged tempo of her breathing, knowing her heartbeat wasn't any steadier. Finally, he handed the box back to her.

She took it carefully, so their hands did not touch, and he smiled.

"Well?" she asked, dropping the box back into her cart.

"Oh, very nutritious. Salt. Sodium. Monosodium glutamate. Fried in shortening. What every American loves."

"And how do you eat?" She looked over the contents of his cart and made a derisive sound. "Rice? Broccoli? What is that weird-looking thing?"

"Fresh ginger."

"Ah." She went back to her examination of his selection of food, wrinkling her nose in a most delightful way.

"And what is that?" she asked, pointing at a square package. "Toe food?"

"Tofu," he corrected her. "Bean curd. High protein. Low fat."

"Yuck." She made a face, then wiggled a finger at another package. "Fish?"

There was a teasing sparkle in her blue eyes when she looked up at him. "Don't you know those things are full of nasty chemicals?"

He chuckled. "Probably fewer than what they put in your foods to preserve them."

"Don't you eat anything good?"

"Do you not?" he returned.

Cockily, she looked up at him. "Of course. I know where the greatest hamburgers in town are sold. And where to find the best pizzas."

"Fast food."

"That's the way I live. Fast. On the run. Which means I either grab something at a restaurant or buy food I can prepare quickly. If I can't zap it in the microwave or get it out of a box or a can, it just won't do."

"Perhaps you need to take time, slow down a little. Consider what you are doing to your body."

"You're one of those health freaks, aren't you?"

He had a feeling she'd like to categorize him as a freak, a nut. He knew he would find it easier if he could dismiss her as an airhead. But she wasn't. And he wasn't about to give her an easy out, either. He shook his head. "No. My father is one of those Americans who loves steak and potatoes and greasy hamburgers, and every so often even I get an urge for one. But my mother's influence has been very strong in my life. Through her, I have learned to appreciate the flavor and beauty of a meal prepared with fresh foods, to care what I put into my body."

"So, we're different," she said. "You're yin and I'm yang. Or something like that."

He smiled at her mix up of the terms. "Or something like that."

"Opposites."

"In many ways."

"If we were around each other very much, we'd probably get on each other's nerves."

"Probably." Eric knew she was certainly doing something to his nerves right now. Never in his life had he felt so edgy, like a tiger circling a tigress, afraid to make the wrong move yet wanting to claim her.

He could tell by the way she kept licking her lips, looking at his mouth, then away, that she was remembering the kiss they'd shared the week before. Oh, they were opposites, all right. What neither of them had dared to say was that opposites attract.

And he was attracted. He hadn't expected to find a woman he could care about here in Ann Arbor, hadn't been looking for one. Now that he'd met Ashley, though, he knew he'd forever regret it if he did not pursue her, did not try to discover how deeply he could come to care for her. She would not make it easy for him, he knew, but he was a patient man. He was certain he intrigued her as much as she intrigued him, and he would find the right time to push their attraction a little, until she stopped resisting.

Ashley deliberately looked down the aisle. She knew if she kept talking, she was going to say or do something stupid again. What she needed to do was get away from him. Far away.

"Well, I'd better get going," she said, straightening her cart. "Thanks again."

"It was nothing."

"See you around?"

"See you around," he repeated.

She didn't look back until she reached the end of the aisle. Then, just before she made the turn, she did chance a glance.

He was gone. The aisle was empty, the man in black only a memory.

She sighed, suddenly feeling very lonely and empty herself, and as quickly as she could, she checked out. It wasn't until she was back at her apartment and halfway through putting her groceries away that she heard Eric go into his apartment. And it wasn't until the next morning that she realized she'd forgotten to buy any peanut butter, bread, or milk.

Over the next month she and Eric saw each other sporadically, twice meeting in the hallway, once down in the laundry area. They exchanged only a few words each time. Hellos. How are yous. Trees are beautiful this fall, aren't they? That was all.

Ashley hated and loved those moments. For days afterward she would remember everything he'd said, how he'd looked and how he'd looked at her. And she'd wonder if he noticed her cheeks got pink every time she saw him, or if he could tell her legs were shaking and that she was trembling inside. She felt like a lovesick teenager, and it bothered her. She also felt more alive than she had in years, maybe in all of her life.

In late October the Ann Arbor *News* had an article announcing the opening of Eric's dojo. It listed his accomplishments, and she was duly impressed. Not only was the man a martial-arts expert, he had a degree in Oriental languages.

Beside the article there was a picture of him, dressed in black, as usual. He looked as sexy and mysterious as ever, and even knowing it was foolish, she cut out the photo and saved it.

Two days later she found an invitation to an open house at the dojo slipped under her door. She supposed he'd given one to everyone in the apartment building, yet she couldn't stop herself from staring at it as though it were a personal request for her presence. For a short while she contemplated going, then her father called.

"Your mother's had a relapse," he said.

"Did she try anything?"

"She was talking about it, so I admitted her."

"Should I come home?"

"No. I just thought you should know."

"She's in Sweet Haven?"

"Yes."

"I'll send her a card."

"You do that."

He sighed, and she knew the burden he carried. It didn't seem fair, and she ached for him. Perhaps he'd never had a lot of time for her, and on occasion she suspected he wished she'd never been born, but she understood. Because of her, his dreams had never come true, none of them. Because of her, he had a wife in and out of hospitals.

"I might be transferring to Chicago," she said,

though she'd been going to wait until Thanksgiving to tell him.

He truly sounded excited for her, asking her all sorts of questions, and they talked for some time. After she'd hung up, though, she felt guilty for not at least feigning more concern for her mother. Yet what could she have said? She gave up hope long ago that her mother would get better. Hospital stays had become a part of her life, the psychotherapy and drug treatments sometimes helping but never curing. She'd be there for a week, maybe longer. Just enough to drain her father, financially and emotionally.

If they were lucky, Ashley thought, this Thanksgiving her mother would be in one of her up moods. In fact, if Evelyn Kehler was really up, she might even be glad to see her daughter.

But Ashley doubted that. What Evelyn Kehler wanted to see was her son, her beloved Jack.

"He's gone, Mom," Ashley whispered, the words spoken to no one. Then she looked at the telephone and smiled. She couldn't help her mother, but one day soon she was going to help her father fulfill his dreams.

"I promised you I would," she said aloud, and crossed her heart as she had when she was a child. "And I will."

After that, she decided it wouldn't be wise to go to Eric's open house. Why play with fire? Like it or not, she was attracted to the man. If she went, who knew what might happen? She couldn't afford to get distracted from her goal. Not now. Not when she was so close.

She spent even more time than ever at the office, and finding a moment to eat wasn't easy. Still, every time she stopped for a hamburger or put a piece of frozen chicken in the microwave, she thought of Eric and felt a tinge of guilt over the high fat and sodium intake of her diet.

So she started buying more vegetables. The kind that were pre-cut and sliced. Fast-food vegetables. And she occasionally ordered a salad.

She certainly wasn't gaining any weight on her diet. "Weight doesn't have time to catch up with you," Charlie would tell her.

Luck, however, did catch up with her.

Bad luck.

It was a Tuesday morning, the first week in November. When she left for work, she forgot part of a proposal she'd worked on the night before at her apartment. It was ten o'clock before she noticed, and with a meeting scheduled for eleven o'clock with the clients, she knew there was nothing to do but go back and get the missing section.

It wouldn't have taken long if her car hadn't decided to stop running five blocks from the apartment building. She was relieved when two men stopped and helped her push her car to the curb so it was out of the lane of traffic. She thanked them both, but declined each of their offers to drive her to her apartment.

One thing her mother had taught her was not to take rides with strangers.

And it was a beautiful day. "We won't have many more like this," she told the men. "I'll just walk."

She could call a cab from her apartment to take her back to work. Her car would have to be dealt with in the afternoon, when she had the time.

It all would have worked out just fine if she hadn't been in her usual hurry and hadn't decided to take a shortcut through an alley.

And if in that alley, she hadn't run into two teen-age boys.

FIVE

Eric entered the apartment building at 10:45 that morning. The moment he stepped through the outside doors, he sensed something wasn't right. Normally, the building was quiet at this hour, unless Charlie was working on one of his renovation projects. What Eric heard wasn't a sound Charlie would be making.

It was more like crying. Ragged, barely audible crying.

He stopped dead still and listened, zeroing in on the exact location of the sound. Quietly, cautiously, he moved toward it.

He found Ashley sitting on the third step of the stairwell, hunched over, her legs drawn close to her body and one arm wrapped around them. The other arm lay across her knees, her face pressed to that hand. Most of her hair had come loose from its twist and dangled in a golden veil, nearly hiding her face from his view.

Her short gray skirt had dirt marks on it, and starting just below scraped knees, her nylons were badly run. With her mouth against the back of her hand, she was trying to muffle her crying, the sound coming out closer to a whimper.

Staring at her, Eric felt her despair, and it tore at his insides. This wasn't the flurry of energy who lived next door to him, wasn't the sparkle of sunshine who heated and aroused him every time they met. The zest had been taken from her, leaving a weeping shadow.

In an instant he scanned the stairwell for signs of another person, then he closed the distance between them. "What happened?" he asked softly, crouching in front of her. He wanted to take her into his arms, yet held back, ready to protect her if her assailant reappeared.

She tensed at the sound of his voice, her head jerking up, her eyes wide with fear. Then he saw recognition in her gaze, and her fear turned to anguish. Closing her eyes, she dropped her head forward again. She drew in a ragged breath, a shudder rocking her body as she fought for emotional control.

"They . . ."

It was all she managed to say before she bit her lower lip and squeezed her lids tighter.

She was drawing into herself, and the fear twisting in his gut took another turn, his mind picturing the worst. He felt a raging anger but forced himself to remain calm, for her sake. Gently, he touched her shoulder. "What did they do to you?"

He was relieved to see she didn't draw back but actually leaned toward his hand. "They..." she repeated, and once again looked at him, her eyes a liquid blue.

"It is all right," he said soothingly, brushing the backs of his fingers over her tear-dampened cheek. "You are all right now. Just tell me what happened."

She nodded, blinking back more tears, and he could tell she was gaining control. Another ragged breath, and she managed to talk. "They took my purse."

"And?" His gaze dropped to her dirt-streaked skirt and skinned knees.

"And I tried to stop them." She sniffled. "They were kids. Teenagers. I never expected ... I mean ..." She blew out a frustrated breath and finished. "They pushed me down."

Again she paused, and he gave her a moment to gather herself before prodding her. "And?"

"And one of them kicked me."

She straightened some, sitting back more on the step. "The kid kicked me. One of them grabbed my purse, the other pushed me down and kicked me. I skinned my knees and my hand—" She showed him the palm of her right hand; the heel was torn and bloody and covered with grit and dirt. Then she touched one of her skinned knees. "Ran a brand-new pair of nylons."

She swore, and Eric smiled, preferring her anger to the whipped image he'd walked in on. But he was still concerned. "Did they do anything else?"

She looked surprised by the idea. "No. When the one pushed me down, I started yelling. I mean, when I hit that pavement, I was mad. Really mad. That's when he kicked me. After that, they took off . . . with my purse, of course."

She sighed, but he was relieved. She'd been mugged, but it could have been worse . . . much worse. "Where did the kid kick you?"

She touched her skirt, along the side of her left thigh, where the dirt marks were the worst. She grimaced when she saw them. Again she swore, then sighed and looked back at Eric. "What a day. First, I screw up and leave my presentation at home, then my car quits running. Now this. Not that they got a lot of money, but besides my wallet, I had my checkbook in my purse. My credit cards. Keys. I can't even get into my apartment."

With a wave of her right hand she motioned down the stairs toward the door to the first floor, then frowned at the pain the motion caused. "Charlie's not even here. No one is." She glanced at her watch and laughed ruefully. "And I'm supposed to be giving a presentation in five minutes."

"Well, you are not going to be giving any presentation in five minutes," Eric said. "But I can get you into your apartment."

"You have a key?"

He smiled and helped her to her feet. "No, but I can get you in."

"How?" She didn't resist as he slipped his arm around her and helped her up the stairs to the second floor.

"Trade secret."

"Learned from being a ninja or from working with the police?"

She was feeling better, he thought. Her curiosity was overriding her fear and pain. "Neither," he said. "This secret is something most two-bit hoods know."

"Oh, that's reassuring."

Instead of taking her to her apartment, he steered her toward his. He didn't know what she might have available to clean her scrapes; he did know what he had.

She tensed as he pulled out his key. "Don't you have the wrong apartment? I'm one more door down."

"First stop is here." He unlocked his door and pushed it wide. "Here we get that hand of yours and your knees cleaned up. *Then* we get you into your place."

Ashley knew she should say no, but she wasn't quite up to arguing. Not yet. Not when Eric's arm around her waist felt so good, when his body was so solid and reassuring, and when being with him seemed so right.

Maybe it wasn't wise, but at the moment, she needed him. In the last hour she'd experienced too many emotions. Irritation first, at herself for forgetting the papers for her meeting; frustration when her car broke down; then fear and helplessness.

She should have been able to defend herself in that alley, but she hadn't. They might have been teenagers, but they'd pushed her around like a rag doll. She knew what Eric had wanted to know when he'd kept prodding her to go on with her story. He'd wanted to know if she'd been raped.

Actually, not until she'd gotten into the apartment building and been searching for someone to help her had she realized how helpless she would have been if the boys had wanted more than just her purse. It was then that her legs had refused to carry her any farther, when all she could do was sit on the stairs and cry.

Eric had appeared only minutes later, coming out of nowhere like an angel of mercy, or maybe a knight in shining armor—armor that consisted of his usual black sweatpants and sweatshirt, along with a light-weight black jacket. One moment she'd been fearful and alone, the next he'd been beside her, comforting her and giving her strength.

He would never know how good it had been to look up and find him crouched in front of her. And she hoped he never guessed how much, at that moment, she'd wanted to throw herself into his arms and never let him go.

After he closed the door behind them, he took off his running shoes, so she did the same with her heels. Then he guided her across the room to his breakfast bar. "Let me help you with your coat," he said, unbuttoning it even as he spoke.

She watched as he began releasing the buttons, then she looked up at his face—at his mouth. His lips were pressed together in concentration, and she remembered how they'd felt the night they'd been pressed against hers.

Firm.

Warm.

Taking in a quick breath, she closed her eyes, willing away the memory.

She felt him start to slip off her coat, and she opened her eyes again, helping him while keeping her palm protected as the sleeve passed over the scraped area. With his help she then got up on one of his barstools.

As she leaned against the breakfast bar, a lethargic tiredness swept over her, draining her of all energy. Wearily, she looked at the telephone sitting on the counter. "I should call my office," she said, as much to herself as to him. "Let them know what happened to me."

"Go ahead," he offered. "And once we have those scrapes cleaned up, we need to call the police."

She liked the way he'd said "we," including himself. At the moment she needed Eric.

He headed for a room that she was certain was his bedroom, since his apartment appeared to be a mirror image of hers. Pausing at the doorway, he glanced back at her. The look in his eyes was warm and tender, and slowly his gaze traveled from her face down over the gray jacket of her suit, her skirt, to her stockinged toes. Despite the weariness that had sapped her energy, she felt something come alive deep inside of her.

"To clean your knees," he said, "either you or I will have to take off your nylons. You decide."

The idea of him taking off her pantyhose brought her totally back to life. Suddenly, her pulse was racing, and a silly giddiness was playing through her system.

She had her pantyhose off and stuffed into a pocket of her suit jacket before she picked up the phone and called her office.

Eric was back by the time she hung up. He'd taken his jacket off and was carrying three medium-sized wide-mouthed jars, each with a white label with Japanese characters drawn on it.

"I lucked out," she said, watching him set the jars on the end of the counter. "I was supposed to make a presentation this morning to the bigwigs of VanGuard Construction. I don't know if you've been following the news about them, but they're the company that built the house where the balcony collapsed, injuring three people."

"Ah, yes, I have read about that." Eric nodded as he went to a cupboard and got out a bowl.

"Anyway," she went on, turning slightly on her stool so she could watch him. "They want our company to get out some PR and fast, so their image isn't ruined. Then they want to follow that up with some long-term PR. That's why I stayed up most of the night working on a proposed game plan. How I handle this is really important to both VanGuard and to my career, which is one reason I was so upset a few minutes ago. I thought I'd really blown it. Only I didn't."

As Eric ran water into the bowl, he glanced at her, his expression questioning.

She explained. "Seems their lawyers wanted to see them this morning, so VanGuard called and canceled at the last minute."

"Ah, that is good, then. I am glad." From a drawer

he took a towel, then brought it and the bowl with warm water over to the three jars on the counter.

"I'm glad too." Curiously, she eyed the jars. "What's in those?"

"Wonder cures my mother creates."

"Your mother?" Ashley kept staring at the jars. "Is she a doctor or something?"

"A something. Trust me," he said. "You will love these salves." He reached for her scraped hand and turned it, carefully, so her palm was up.

"Trust you." She gritted her teeth and flinched as he touched the raw flesh with the dampened end of the towel. "I've heard that line before."

"And?" He glanced at her face, a sparkle of amusement in his dark eyes.

"And every time I have, I've regretted it." She kept her gaze on his bent head and tried to ignore the smarting pain of her hand.

He chuckled and stopped dabbing at her palm. A glance down, and she realized the scrape was clean. "You did that fast."

"Speedy Newman at your service." He reached over and opened one of the jars.

It was half-filled with a dark, murky cream that smelled terrible. As he scooped up a small amount with two fingers, she wrinkled her nose. "Are you really going to put that on my hand?"

"Yes." He chuckled and dabbed a bit onto the scrape. "Believe me, in a few minutes when that hand starts feeling better, and when you see how fast it heals, you will be begging me for your own jar of this stuff."

She sniffed again and doubted anything would make her beg for the contents of that jar. "So, what's in it?"

He closed the jar and opened another. "Mostly natural herbs and ground roots. Maybe a powdered bat wing or two."

"Powdered bat wing?" She eyed him suspiciously. "Are you pulling my leg?"

He glanced down at her legs, then smiled. "Not yet." He scooped up a little of the second jar's contents. "Actually, all of these salves are made from recipes that have been handed down from generation to generation. I have helped my mother mix them, but I do not think you would recognize any of the ingredients. Mostly they are roots that are common in Japan. You will not find too many here at your local market or pharmacy."

The second salve at least smelled better, and by the time he'd rubbed on the third, her palm was feeling better. In fact, it was feeling quite good, she realized. She was no longer even thinking of the pain but beginning to respond on a different level to the gentle, rotating motion of his fingers on her palm. She was relieved when he released her hand. Another minute and he would have had her purring . . . or groaning.

Cautiously, she moved her hand, amazed by the change that had occurred. "You're turning me into a believer," she admitted, able to make a fist without it hurting. "And don't say, 'I told you so.' "

He grinned as he stepped back so he could see her knees. Taking a clean section of the towel, he began the same process with those scrapes. Again, in the beginning, she gritted her teeth. And again, by the time he'd applied the second salve, the pain was gone, and she was more aware of him than of what he was doing.

Simply being around him was enough to put her system on alert. Being touched by him, stroked, caressed, sent tingling sensations dancing through her body.

In silence he concentrated on his job, carefully covering every inch of the scrapes. As he worked, she stared at the top of his head, his thick, shaggy black hair begging for her touch. She fought the urge.

Keeping her hands by her sides, she looked around his apartment.

The layout was the same as hers—a living room/dining area, kitchen with a breakfast bar, bathroom, and bedroom. His looked different, though. Her apartment had a busy, hectic feel, her furniture covered with flowery patterns, every tabletop and flat surface holding at least one knick-knack and usually more. The atmosphere in Eric's apartment was open and airy. Quiet. In his dining area a low black enameled table was surrounded by bright, colorful pillows, not chairs, and the sum contents of his living room were a low black leather couch and matching chair, a bright red enameled coffee table, and a state-of-the-art television/entertainment center. On the walls were framed black-and-white photos and stylistic Japanese paintings, each a combination of stark simplicity and intriguing depth.

Actually, everything about the apartment reflected the simple strength of Eric and the intriguing mystery of him, and she let her gaze drift back to his face.

He was different from anyone she'd ever known—quiet, unassuming, and sure of himself. She had a feeling he was a lot closer to his discovery of enlightenment than she was to a move to Chicago. He wouldn't leave important papers at home, and he wouldn't have been caught off guard by two teenagers.

"I guess I probably should take that class of yours," she said.

He glanced up at her face.

"You know," she continued, "the one you were telling me about some time back. The one for people who just want to learn basic self-defense. If I'd had it, I could have protected myself today."

He studied her, then nodded. "I think it would have made a difference."

The more she thought about the idea, the more she liked it. "I would have loved to put those two punks on their knees. Wouldn't they have been surprised."

"It would have been better for you, and for your knees"—he changed to the next salve—"not to have been in a position where you had to defend yourself at all."

She noted a hint of censure. "Hey, I agree, but what was I to do? My car died on the way here. My other choice was to accept a ride with a man I didn't know. I thought walking was safer."

"To have seen the danger and avoided it would have been safer."

She hated to admit it, but he was probably right. It would have been safer to have taken the longer, more traveled route to her apartment. And if, while taking the shortcut through the alley, she hadn't been thinking about her upcoming presentation, hadn't been worried about getting back to the office, she might have seen the boys in time to take defensive action.

"When I was young," she said, "my brother used to tell me if I'd slow down and think about where I was going, I'd get there faster."

"He was right," Eric said. "Faster and safer."

She grinned. "I thought you ninjas thrived on danger."

"You are talking about the ones you see in the movies or find in fiction. Those writers romanticize the ninja warrior, always having him sneak around in the dark, into this deception and that. They are not the true ninjas."

"And what is the true ninja?"

"A warrior who tries to avoid fighting, who does not dwell on the idea of defeating others or sneaking up on victims in the night."

"And what about when you're sneaking around for the police?"

He smiled. "If I did do such a thing, and I am not saying I do, it would be because what I had been asked to find was very important, and finding it would help a great number of people."

She noticed he wasn't saying he did it, but he also hadn't flatly denied it. So much about him was a mystery. "Why does a man want to be a ninja in the first place?"

"For me, it is to be prepared, to know myself, my strengths and weaknesses . . . to be a *tatsujin*, a complete human being. To be in tune with the universe."

"And what if a person already knows her or his strengths and weaknesses?"

He gazed deep into her eyes. "Do you?"

"I know many of my strengths and weaknesses. I know, for one thing, that I'm a realist, and that I'll probably never be in tune with the universe."

He grinned. "More than likely you will turn the universe upside down." He replaced the lid on the last jar and wiped his hands on the towel. "How do your knees feel?"

"Good." She tried each leg, flinching only when she moved the left. Her thigh was sore where the boy had kicked her.

"Now, we will work on that."

Before she understood what he meant, Eric had stepped closer and touched her thigh right where she'd been kicked, the tips of his fingers slipping up under her skirt. Immediately, she tensed, the muscles between her legs tightening and a crazy giddiness swamping her stomach. Her mind in a whirl, her body suddenly very hot, she covered his hand with hers, stopping him.

He looked up and smiled. "Trust me."

"You said that before," she reminded him, her voice shakier than earlier.

"And did I hurt you?"

"I . . ." She glanced down at her left leg. The sight of Eric's fingers disappearing under her skirt did not help the giddy sensation in her stomach. "I think this is different."

"Just relax," he soothed. "Close your eyes, think of something very pleasant, and give your leg to me."

She was afraid she would soon be giving more than her leg to him.

"All I am going to do," he said softly, reassuringly, "is massage those muscles, get the blood circulating so the damaged tissue can begin to heal."

The way her heart was beating and her pulse was racing, her blood had to be circulating quite rapidly already. Nevertheless, she said nothing. Afraid to speak, she stared into his eyes, his irises and pupils so dark, one melted into the other. In those dusky mirrors she saw a woman hesitant and vulnerable, more afraid of her own reactions than of the man causing them.

She closed her eyes and prayed for the strength to ignore the thoughts that kept jumping into her head. She felt him move his hand higher, farther up under her skirt, and she groaned, more with the agony of ecstasy than because of any pain.

He worked his magic, and she fantasized.

Each caress of his fingers, each stroke of his hand, eased the soreness from her muscles and increased the needs of her body. The awareness coursing through her was driving her wild. Finally, she could take no more.

"No," she murmured, opening her eyes and reaching out to touch his arm.

Eric stopped what he was doing and looked at her. Through her leg, he could feel her heat and tension and knew neither had anything to do with pain. No more than the fever burning in him had anything to do with physical exertion.

From the moment he'd seen her on the stairs, he'd tried to remain detached and emotionally uninvolved. She was a woman in need of help, and he could give her that help. It was not right to ask for more. Not at this moment.

Only his body didn't seem to understand. Simply rubbing her leg was causing him physical problems. And as hard as he tried to keep his thoughts pure and impersonal, it was impossible. All he could think of was the softness of her skin, the sweet smell of her, and how beautiful she would be without any clothes on.

As he gazed into her eyes, he knew she wanted him as much as he wanted her. With his free hand he reached up and touched the side of her face. She drew in a shaky breath and let her fingers glide up his sleeves to his shoulders. Slowly, they leaned toward each other, drawn by some invisible force beyond their control.

Eric wasn't sure if her lips touched his first, or if he initiated the kiss. He knew only that the moment his mouth covered hers, a sense of completeness swept over him, and there was no turning back. Each kiss was a giving and a receiving, an exploration and a sensual delight. Her mouth was firm yet soft, her taste sweet and satisfying.

The slightest touch with his tongue, and she opened to him, inviting him in. He entered hesitantly, then grew bolder. Each thrust of his tongue she parried with her own, teasing him to distraction.

She was hot and responsive, and he slid his hand higher on her thigh, pushing her skirt and slip up to her hips and finding the edge of silky panties. Pulling her forward on the stool, he parted her knees and wedged himself between her legs.

He heard her take in a quick breath, and her hands tightened on his shoulders. For a moment she remained tense; then he felt her resistance melt. As she wrapped her arms around him, the front of her suit jacket touched the front of his sweatshirt, and her breasts became a soft cushioning between them.

He knew all possibilities for self-control were slipping away, more primitive urges taking over. He was hot and hard and aching for the relief he would find with her. Every basic male instinct urged him on, begged him to remove her clothing and his. Only years of disciplined training and the realization that she was probably not reacting as she normally would held him in check.

With a reluctant groan he ended the kiss and stepped back. She tried to hold him to her, but he quickly pulled her slip and skirt into place, not daring to glance at the silky panties he'd touched or the sweet, tempting mound they covered.

She looked at him through passion-filled eyes, her confusion evident. She said nothing, but he could tell from her uneven breathing and the flush of her skin that she was highly aroused. How far she would have let him go, he didn't know, and he wouldn't find out today.

"Your leg," he finally managed to say, "should feel better now."

"My leg." She repeated the words as though in a trance.

"Where the boy kicked you."

"Yes, my leg." She looked down at her skirt, then she closed her eyes. He saw her shudder.

"We should call the police now," he went on. "Report what happened."

Ashley nodded, keeping her eyes closed. She understood what he was saying. What she didn't understand was what had just happened between them. One moment he'd been massaging her leg, the next they'd been kissing. No, it had been more than kissing. She'd been ready to give herself to him, to spread her legs and make love with him.

The need flooding through her scared her. Every nerve ending in her body was on edge, while frustration battled with reason. This was the second time since she'd met Eric that while part of her was begging to go on, another part was thanking him for stopping.

She certainly wouldn't have called a halt, and that alone scared her. What was it about Eric? She wasn't a woman who easily gave herself to a man, and she'd never made love with a man she barely knew. The few relationships she'd had were exactly that, relationships, developed over months and based on friendship, not lust.

With Eric . . .

She felt rather than heard him move away. For a moment longer she kept her eyes closed; then she opened them. He was gathering the jars of salve, the towel, and the bowl of water he'd used to clean her scrapes. His actions were deliberate, and she might have thought he was totally unaffected by what had just happened between them if he hadn't glanced her way.

His look was hungry—yearning—and he quickly turned away.

SIX

Ashley noticed that Eric didn't touch her again after that, but he did help her call the police, asking for one man specifically, a Lieutenant Pease. She gave the lieutenant a description of the two boys. He said he'd send an officer out to talk to her, but he didn't give her much hope that she'd ever see her purse again.

After the call Eric opened the door to her apartment. He did it with amazing ease; then he left.

Left her alone to remember everything that had happened that morning—her fears, her passion, and her embarrassment. Left her aching for what might have been and confused by her reactions. Most of all, he left her wondering what was to come.

She didn't see him again that day, though. Or the next.

Two nights later, close to ten o'clock, there was a knock at her door. Without knowing why, she hoped it was Eric. She'd often heard him come home at that hour. When she opened her door, however, Charlie was standing in the hallway. In one hand he held her stolen purse.

"Mrs. Wyconski brought it to bingo tonight," he said. "She knew I'd be there. Said she found it in the Dumpster when she took out her garbage this morning and could tell by the address that it belonged to someone in my building. I'm afraid your money and credit cards are gone."

So were her checkbook and keys, all of the pens and pencils she always carried, and a pack of gum. Actually, that her wallet was still there, along with her driver's license, proof of insurance, and a picture of her brother, was amazing. Not that she'd be driving her car until she got it out of the repair shop.

The boys had also left her makeup, her emergency supply of tampons, and the notebook she used to jot down ideas. She supposed, all in all, it could have been worse. Other than the cash she'd been carrying, which wasn't much, she'd lost little. A few phone calls had closed her checking account and notified the credit card companies of the theft. The biggest bother was the nuisance of having to replace everything.

"How are the knees and hand?" Charlie asked.

She showed him her hand and pulled up her skirt so he could see her knees. "It's amazing, Charlie. Two days and they're almost entirely healed. If you hadn't seen how they looked that morning, I doubt you'd believe how bad they were. I tell you, if Eric ever patents those salves and sells them, he'll be a millionaire."

She could have added that he could also make millions from his massages. His fingers had worked magic. Her thigh was a little tender and showed some bruising, but nothing like she'd expected. She'd gotten worse bumping into the edge of a desk.

"Police have any leads on those hoodlums who attacked you?" Charlie asked, showing no inclination to leave.

"I looked at some mug shots yesterday, but I didn't see anyone who resembled those boys." She shook her head. "I doubt I'll ever see them again."

"Don't know what this world is coming to. And this is considered a good neighborhood." He sighed and gave her shoulder a gentle squeeze. "You just take care of yourself, okay? Don't go getting into a situation like that again."

"I won't," she promised. She certainly didn't intend to. Once had been frightening enough.

Charlie glanced toward Eric's apartment. "You ever thought about having him teach you some self-defense?"

"I've thought about it." Thought and thought, and decided going to one of his classes wasn't a wise idea. Every time they touched, things seemed to happen.

"Heard he's pretty good," Charlie went on. "Seventh-degree black belt, whatever that means."

"Probably means he's pretty good." She smiled and started to close the door. "Thanks again, Charlie, for bringing my purse, and thank Mrs. ah . . ."

"Wyconski. I will, that I will. You take care now, don't work too hard."

"I won't," she said, and laughed when, even as she was shutting the door, Charlie repeated his suggestion that she go see Eric and learn how to protect herself.

When she came home the next night, she wasn't sure if Charlie or Eric had left the flyer about the classes Eric offered. But when she ran into Eric that Saturday, he confirmed that he was the one who'd slipped the paper under her door. "You really should learn some self-defense," he said.

"I don't have time." To emphasize her point, she tapped the briefcase she carried. She was on her way to the office.

He glanced at it, then at her legs. "How are your knees?"

"Low blow," she grumbled, knowing exactly what he was saying.

"I can teach you many things."

She could imagine.

"It is better to be in control than controlled."

Control was the problem. Self-control. Hers. His. "I'll think about it," she said.

He bowed slightly. "I will await the day you honor my dojo with your presence."

"Eric . . ." she started, wanting to explain her confusion and fears. But what could she say? I'm afraid of how you make me feel? I'm afraid I might get to like you?

He wouldn't understand.

"I'll see you around," she finally said, and hurried toward the stairs.

She didn't see Eric for the next two weeks, mostly because she spent so many hours at the office, but she often thought of him and her promise. He saw to that. One day she came home to find a package at her door. When she opened it, she discovered three small jars of the same salves he'd used on her cuts and scrapes, along with instructions on how and when to use each.

Another day it was a newspaper article slipped under her door, its topic attacks on women and what women should do to protect themselves. Eric had highlighted the sentence suggesting learning martial arts.

And when she did her laundry, she saw the flyer he'd tacked up on the wall, boldly advertising the Eric Newman Martial Arts Academy. She knew from the address that it wasn't far from the apartment building. In fact, it wasn't far from her office.

The day she drove by his dojo, she told herself she was just curious. And it wasn't really that far out of her way home. Two nights later, when she stopped, she also told herself she was simply curious.

She'd worked overtime trying to find the right wording for the press releases she was preparing for the VanGuard Construction company. Though it was late, several cars were parked in the parking lot. She knew Eric taught a class at this time.

She would just take a peek, she reasoned. Poke

her head in and see what a martial-arts dojo was like. Maybe watch for a minute or two. That was all.

A light snow was falling, and the moment Ashley got out of her car, she was hit by a gust of bitter cold. Head bent low, a thick scarf pulled up around her face, she hurried to the door of the building. Once inside, she was assailed by the smell of sweaty bodies and the sounds of grunts and groans.

For a moment she stood where she was, looking around. The reception area wasn't very big and included a few chairs, a coatrack with about a half-dozen coats hanging on it, and what seemed to be a combination registration counter and sales shop. Since no one was around, she proceeded on through a doorway, following the grunts and groans.

She stepped into a large open room and again stopped to look around. Along one wall a long bench was separated from the huge mat-covered floor area by a low wooden barrier and a few support beams. A young woman sat on the far end of the bench, a middle-aged man toward the middle. Both were watching the mat where four men and two women, ranging in age from mid-twenties to early sixties, were paired up and practicing various moves. All six were wearing white uniforms, but three had green belts, two had brown belts, and one had a plain black belt.

Ashley focused on the one man on the mat who was dressed in black. Not only was his uniform different, so was his black belt. His, she noted, had several red and gold markings on it.

He walked behind the students, watching each

one, stopping now and then to make a comment or demonstrate a procedure. Fascinated, she walked into the room and sat on the end of the bench nearest the door. As she removed her scarf and slipped out of her coat, she kept her gaze on Eric.

She knew the moment he saw her, a tingle of awareness spiraling down her spine as their gazes locked. She smiled. He gave the slightest of nods, then turned his attention to the next student.

She was disappointed that he didn't come over to talk to her. Yet, in a way, she was also glad he didn't. Simply looking into his eyes had been enough to send her pulse rate soaring. If he'd made a fuss about her presence, she probably would have turned into a gibbering idiot and would have had to leave right away.

As it was, she stayed . . . purely out of curiosity, she once again told herself.

Soon, however, curiosity turned to intrigue. He taught an escape, and she jotted down the procedure as the others paired up and practiced on each other. He demonstrated a kick, and she made a sketch. Then he clapped his hands, and his students moved toward the edges of the mat, leaving the center clear. One student remained, the man wearing the black belt.

He and Eric stepped toward the center of the mat. They bowed to each other, then Ashley watched in stunned astonishment as her quiet, compassionate, mild-mannered neighbor changed before her eyes.

The man with the plain black belt threw a blow. Like an elusive shadow, Eric was no longer where he'd been standing but was suddenly beside the man, trapping his extended arm and bringing him down to his knees. The man quickly regained his feet and grabbed Eric's wrist. Before Ashley could take in a breath, Eric was again beside his attacker, his captured hand already free. With lightning speed he struck his own blow, spun, and kicked.

Each maneuver Eric executed thrilled Ashley. In front of her was disciplined, controlled power. He moved like the wind—like a sleek black panther—circling his opponent, slipping in and out, hitting, jabbing, and kicking, or totally avoiding counter-attacks.

He had told her what he was not; she had never understood what he was.

The duel ended. Eric knelt on the mat, and his students knelt behind him. Together they bowed toward the distant wall and chanted words she did not understand. They clapped their hands sharply twice, bowed again, gave one more sharp clap and follow-up bow.

As Eric stood, he watched Ashley stand and pull on her coat. The way she was hurrying, he knew he had to get to her quickly, before she slipped away. Barely acknowledging comments his students made, he crossed the mat and vaulted the low safety barrier. He reached her side just as she buttoned the last button.

"Do not run off," he said softly, and saw her catch a breath before she looked at him.

The guilt in her eyes said that was exactly what she'd planned. She might have still left, if his students hadn't helped by picking that moment to all congregate at the doorway.

"It's late," she said nervously. "I should be going."

"Is it still snowing outside?"

She nodded. "We've probably gotten two or three inches."

"Would you be so kind as to give me a ride home?"

He hoped the request would work, would keep her around after his students left. His wanting her to stay was only partly because she filled him with excitement and pleasure when he was with her. She had been avoiding him at the apartment building, and he truly believed she needed the training he could provide. She had come to his dojo that night, but from her actions, he didn't think she would come again, not unless he could convince her that she was safe with him.

"You need a ride?" she asked, sounding surprised.

"I walked over. I could walk back"— he usually did—"but I thought, if you are going that way . . . ?"

He let the idea hang, not pushing it. The decision had to be hers.

"Sure, I guess," she said finally.

"Good." He leaped back over the barrier onto the mat. "I have got to put a few things away, then lock up. I hope you do not mind."

"No, of course not." She anxiously looked toward the door. The others were beginning to leave.

He had little to do to close up, but he took his time. He wanted the others to be gone, and he needed to calm the racing of his heart. He hadn't expected to look up and see Ashley sitting on the bench. Now that she was there, he had to move cautiously.

Finally, he came back to where she waited near the door. She straightened as he approached. "All ready?" she asked.

"Almost." He slipped past her and went to the reception counter. There, he thumbed through his scheduling book, as though checking something. His back to her, he asked, "So are you here to sign up for some classes in self-defense?"

"I've, ah, been thinking about it."

"Still just thinking?" Slowly, he turned to face her. "I understand they still have not found the boys who mugged you."

"No, they haven't."

"You know, it could have been more than your purse they were after," he went on, wanting her to understand his concern. "You could have ended up with a lot worse than a bruise and a few scrapes."

"I know." Gazing at him, her eyes a smoky blue, she sighed. "I got the point of that article you left. And you're probably right. I should learn some ways to defend myself."

"It could save your life."

"It's just that . . ." She hesitated, looking away, then back again. "I'm not much of an athlete. I mean, I used to be pretty good at gymnastics when I was younger, but after the accident, I just . . ." Her voice trailed off.

"What accident?"

"I was in a car crash," she said, and sighed again. "It's something I don't like to talk about."

"You were seriously injured?" He had never seen any signs of a disability.

"No. I hardly even got a scratch, but ever since then I haven't had any desire to get involved in any competitive sport."

He sensed she was wrong, that the accident had harmed her in some way, but he honored her request and did not ask her to talk about it. At the moment it was more important to convince her to take his class in self-defense.

"You would have no problem here," he assured her. "I do not teach competitive martial arts. My students are not being prepared for tournaments. Here, you learn the art of survival, street survival. It is not a game. On the street there is no 'second place.' You either go home healthy and happy, or you don't."

"I'd just as soon go home happy," she said.

He had a feeling, the way she was hanging near the door, that included tonight. That she was so edgy bothered him. "Relax, Ashley," he said softly. "I am not going to attack you."

"I never thought you would," she said, but stayed near the door.

"Of course." He leaned back against the counter, smiling slightly. "Still, you are afraid of me. Is it because of what happened in my apartment?"

Nervously, she licked her lips. "I . . . What happened that morning was . . ."

She paused, and he finished for her. "Unexpected. Unplanned." He lowered his voice, so his words were barely above a whisper. "Yet not unwanted. Would you agree?"

"I didn't want it to happen," she insisted, her cheeks taking on more color.

"Yet it did." He frowned. "Have you decided it was all my fault?"

"No," she said quickly. "I . . ." She lifted her hands, as though about to make a point, then let them drop back to her sides. "I don't know what came over me that morning. I must have been in some sort of shock or something."

"And now?"

It was her turn to frown. "Now?"

"You are afraid to come close to me. Why?"

"I'm not afraid," she said and stepped away from the door toward him. "I just thought we were ready to go. I didn't know you'd want to have a long conversation."

"Not a long one."

He made a sweeping gesture with his hand, indicating he wanted her to come even closer. For a moment she stood where she was, then she walked over to him, stopping an arm's length away. "Is this what you want?"

He straightened, moving away from the wall and closer. Immediately, she took a step back, and he smiled. "You are definitely afraid of me."

"I am not." She lifted her chin and stepped forward again, leaving only inches between them. "If you want to play games, fine."

He willed himself not to touch her. "Sometimes games are necessary."

"Like the game you and that other man with the black belt played tonight? If you did that to impress me with your abilities, you succeeded."

"That was not a game. That was a training session.

At the end of each class I work out with one of the higher-ranked students. It gives them the practice they need and shows the newer students what they can hope to achieve in the future."

Yet she was right, Eric thought. It had been, in part, a show for her. Instead of playing his usual role of attacker, testing his student's defensive abilities, he'd purposefully decided to reverse the roles so Ashley could see what he could do. It was difficult to admit, even to himself, but there was still a bit of the little boy in him who wanted to show off for the girl next door. "So, were you impressed?"

"Very," she admitted. "You're good."

"And now you will sign up for a class?"

"Considering what seems to happen every time we get together, would it be wise?"

Wise? he wondered. Perhaps not. But he knew she needed what he could teach her. All he had to do was control his emotions, and everything would be fine. "When you come here, I will be your sensei. Your teacher. And you will be Ashley-san, one of my students. I would treat you no different from any other student. That I promise."

"No different," she repeated, never looking away from his face, and he prayed for the strength not to let her see how much he wanted to touch her, kiss her.

To his surprise she was the one who reached up and touched him, her fingertips grazing his jaw. "Then I think you have more self-control than I do." Her gaze was unwavering, though her voice was shaky. "Eric, I don't know what to do."

He shuddered, feeling his self-control slipping. Tentatively, he touched her shoulders, her wool coat coarse against his palms. "If it helps," he said, "neither do I."

"I should stay far away from you."

"Miles and miles away."

"Avoid seeing you."

"You have been doing a pretty good job lately."

"Not good enough. I couldn't stay away tonight."

"I am glad." He tightened the pressure of his grip on her shoulders, bringing her closer.

"This will never work," she whispered just before she slid her fingers into his hair.

"Never," he agreed.

Then he kissed her.

It might not have been so bad if it had been a simple kiss, a brushing of lips, over in less than a minute. But with Ashley, as he'd already discovered, one minute was never enough time. Nor two. Nor three. He simply couldn't get enough of her.

And while his mouth pillaged hers, his hands were moving. Across her shoulders. Up to her hair. He pulled out each pin that kept her taffy-colored tresses so neatly confined, and when her hair was loose, he ran his fingers through it, delighting in its silky softness.

She worked on his obi, persistently tugging at the knot until she succeeded in releasing it. The moment his belt dropped to the floor, the jacket of his uniform fell open, and she placed her hands against his stomach.

Reflexively, he sucked in a breath and tightened his

abdominal muscles. Lower, another muscle became painfully hard.

"Sensei," she murmured, kissing him on one bared shoulder and working her hands up to his chest. "You have a wonderful body."

"So do you, Ashley-san." He pulled her hair back and nipped at her earlobe, catching a pearl stud between his teeth. Then he trailed little kisses down her neck to the collar of her coat. "So do you."

Finding the buttons of her coat, he released them, one by one, and slid his hands under the heavy wool, only to run into the buttons of her suit jacket. Frustrated, he nuzzled her neck. "You also wear too many clothes."

"And you have hardly any on."

She slipped her fingers under the elastic waistband of his pants, and he sucked in another quick breath. "Careful," he warned.

"Or?" Boldly, she worked her hands around to the front of his trousers.

"Or you are going to discover just what you do to me."

"And what do I do to you?"

She was teasing him, testing his willpower. The problem was, he wasn't sure just how strong his willpower was. Or how long it was going to last.

"You drive me crazy," he said, "that is what you do. And if you keep that up, in two more seconds you and I are going to be on that mat making love."

"And I would let you," she said with regret, and pulled her hands free. Quickly, she turned away.

"That's why I can't come here, Eric. Can't take classes from you."

Staring at her back, he knew then that she'd been testing him . . . and perhaps herself. For a moment anger darkened his thoughts; then he felt guilt. He'd failed, given in to his desire when she'd wanted him to remain strong.

"We simply need to take safeguards," he said. "Tonight I wanted you here, alone, so we could talk. I wanted to—"

He stopped. He couldn't tell her he'd wanted to prove that she could trust him, wanted to show her that nothing would happen. Something had happened.

But they could stop it from happening again. He was sure of that. "If you take classes, you do not stay after, and I do not ask you to stay after. It is that simple."

She turned back toward him. "None of this is simple."

"It can be." He straightened her coat, then began to rebutton it. "Come on, let us get out of here."

She said nothing, but she watched his face as he worked on each button. Her breathing was shallow, and her cheeks flushed. As soon as he finished with her coat, he picked up his obi and retied it around his uniform, then got his outside jacket and slipped it on. Finally, they were both ready to leave, and he held the door for her before snapping off the lights and locking up.

In her car, as they drove from the dojo to the apartment building, they discussed the weather, what it had cost her to have the timing chain replaced in her car, and how she needed to get a new car one of these days. He knew she was also thinking, coming up with excuses for why his idea wouldn't work. As he walked with her up the stairs to the second floor, he prayed he'd have the right words to convince her it would.

SEVEN

As they reached the second-floor landing, Ashley wondered if Eric had any idea how much she'd wanted to make love with him on that mat . . . or how much her own desire scared her. She'd started her seduction bit to prove his idea of him teacher/her student wouldn't work.

Well, she'd proved it all right. She'd also proved that not seeing him for two weeks hadn't lessened the attraction, hadn't weakened the chemistry. Around Eric, she simply wasn't her normal self. When she was with him, she forgot how important it was to her—and to her father—that she succeed at her job. She forgot the promise she'd made her brother.

"Well, good night," she said as they neared the door to his apartment.

"Good night," he said, but he didn't leave her

there. Never hesitating, he walked on with her to her door.

Quickly, she slipped her key in the lock and turned it. The moment she opened her door, she faced him. "See you around."

She tried to step inside and close the door, but he stopped her. "Ashley, not learning self-defense is foolish."

"Who said I'm not going to learn?"

"I have a class Tuesday and Thursday evenings and Saturday afternoons that is just what you need. Basic self-defense. Nothing more. You will come?"

She knew she couldn't, no more than she could look him in the eyes and lie to him. So she looked at the floor. "Maybe."

"Meaning no." He gave an exasperated sigh. "We cannot go on trying to ignore how we feel. It is not working."

"It will work," she insisted, knowing her voice sounded panicky, yet unable to control it. She forced herself to look back up. "It has to work."

"Why? Why not let what will be, be? Get to know each other. See what happens."

"It wouldn't be—" She stopped herself. Wouldn't be safe? Wise?

How could she explain?

"It would be," he argued. "It is better to discover what is ahead than to hide our heads in the sand."

"I am not hiding my head in the sand. I simply know it wouldn't work between us."

"You are probably right." Just the hint of a smile touched his lips. "Even our hours are in conflict. With me, I am free most mornings but busy most afternoons and evenings."

She jumped at the opportunity to confirm that she had no time for romance. "I'm at the office during the day, and a lot of times late into the evening."

"Late like tonight?"

"Yes."

"And what about tomorrow night?"

Tomorrow was Friday, but that made little difference to her. She often spent her Friday nights and weekends working. "I'm sure I'll be working until . . ." She picked a time that she figured would be too late for him to think of asking her out. "Ten-thirty."

"Good." He smiled in satisfaction. "I will be free by then. We can have a late supper together. Something simple."

"But—" She realized he'd tricked her. Somehow she'd left herself open, and he'd stepped in and backed her into a corner.

"I am really a very good cook," he said, and bowed. "Until tomorrow night then."

"But," she repeated, trying to think of a reason why she couldn't have a late supper with him.

He turned and walked toward his apartment.

"It wouldn't work," she called after him.

He stopped at his door and looked back at her. "That is what we will find out."

The next day Ashley called his dojo and left a message that she was sorry but something had come up, and she couldn't make it. An hour later her secretary brought her a message that Eric had called and said he expected her at eleven. Swearing under her breath, Ashley decided she would go, eat his food, then she would leave. She'd show him she could be in his presence for more than five minutes and not turn into a sex-starved idiot.

She didn't know what came over her every time she was around him, but this time things were going to be different. He wanted to get to know her? Well, she'd tell him about herself. She'd talk about her work until he begged her to shut up and leave.

Grinning with satisfaction, she went back to the brochure she was working on for VanGuard Construction. It wouldn't be the first time she'd scared off a guy with her devotion to her job. Men, she'd learned long ago, liked to talk about themselves, not listen to a woman go on and on about demographics, publics, opinion polls, and media manipulation.

That night she forced herself to stay at her office until ten-thirty, simply because she'd told Eric she'd be there that long, but from eight o'clock on she didn't accomplish a thing. Finally, she slipped the VanGuard file into her drawer, gathered her courage as well as her coat and scarf, and left the building.

She parked her car in the lot across the street from the apartment building and could see the lights on in Eric's apartment. Cautiously, she tiptoed by his door on the way to hers, and once inside, made as little noise as she could. Rebelliously, she wondered what he would do if she just didn't show up.

At eleven o'clock on the dot, he knocked on the

wall between their living rooms, and she knew he knew she was there. Once again that day she swore, then she headed for his apartment.

Her courage abandoned her the moment he opened his door and bowed. Any ideas she'd had of controlling what happened between them disappeared. She was beginning to believe ninjas did possess mystical powers, could cloud a person's thinking, because simply looking into Eric's eyes mesmerized her.

"Ashley-san," he said in his quiet way, his gaze sweeping over her, from her tailored red suit to the toes of her red pumps. "Welcome."

He stepped back, and she managed to enter his apartment, her legs suddenly unstable. Seeing his running shoes by the door, she quickly slipped off her heels, certain she would be better off flat-footed.

The click of the door closing beside her caused her stomach to tighten. How she was going to eat anything, she didn't know.

"Do you want to take off your jacket?" he asked.

"No . . . thank you." She faced him and found him smiling.

"And what are you grinning about?" she asked. She hoped he hadn't guessed her motive for wearing a tailored business suit instead of changing into something more casual and relaxed.

Of course, if he'd read any of the "dress for success" books she had, he knew about "power red" and the psychological effects of a tailored suit, especially for a woman trying to gain control in a business negotiation. Not that this was a business negotiation or that wearing a red suit was helping. Two seconds with Eric, and she felt she'd lost control.

"I am grinning because the color red becomes you," he said without hesitation.

The way he looked at her convinced her that he did know what she was trying to prove. She was also sure that the color black became him. Black jeans. A black turtleneck. Black hair and dark eyes. He was a black panther, all right. Lean and vibrantly poised, waiting for his prey to show a weakness, make a mistake.

Her mistake, she was certain, was in coming. Nervously, she licked her lips.

"I fixed *yosenabe*," he said casually, as though they often met for late-night suppers. He turned toward the kitchen. "Come, I have only a little more to do, and it will be ready."

She followed cautiously. "*Yosenabe?*"

"Translated, it means a bit of everything," he explained. "In Japan it is a popular dish for cold, blustery winter days."

The temperature outside was near freezing, but she was feeling anything but cold. With the soft sounds of Japanese music playing in the background and the air filled with the smells of cooking, Eric's apartment was warm and cozy. Too warm, she decided, undoing the buttons on her suit jacket.

She stopped near the end of the counter, then remembered what had happened between them at that same spot only a little over two weeks before. Quickly, she stepped away. When she looked at him, he was watching her. Once again just the hint of a smile touched his lips.

She pretended she didn't notice and sniffed the air. "Fish?"

"Shellfish," he answered, and showed her the cracked crab and shrimp on his chopping block before dumping them into a kettle on the stove. "Along with clams that are already cooking. I hope you like shellfish."

"I do. Except for raw oysters. I don't like that or sushi." She'd tried both once and each time had nearly gagged.

"No raw oysters or sushi," he promised. He lifted a small stoneware pitcher from a pan of simmering water and set it on the counter to cool. "Did you get a lot of work done tonight?"

"Tons," she lied, and decided he'd just given her the perfect opportunity to bore him with stories about her work.

Leaning back against the breakfast bar, she began to tell him of her day. As she talked, he worked. After a few minutes of cooking, he removed the shrimp, clams, and crab from the kettle on the stove and placed them in a casserole. She continued talking, almost nonstop, as he added cabbage to the broth in the kettle. She told him about the aggressive PR campaign they were waging on behalf of VanGuard Construction, about the press releases she'd done and would be doing to show the steps the company was taking to ensure that such a tragedy didn't happen again, and about the brochures and ads that would go out, all of which she was certain would soon help change the public's perception of VanGuard Construction.

Occasionally, Eric did manage to get a word in to ask a question, showing far more interest than she'd expected . . . or had hoped for. Finally, by the time he'd removed the cabbage from the broth and added what she suspected was tofu, then removed that and poured the broth from the kettle over everything he'd placed in the casserole, she was sure she was getting across to him her devotion to her job.

He carried the casserole out to the dining area, placing it in the center of his low-to-the-floor black table. Then he brought in the stoneware pitcher. He already had two place settings on the table—bright red woven straw mats with a bowl, a tiny teacup, a fork, and chopsticks. Two large silk pillows—one gold and one red—were the only seats available. As Eric knelt on the red one to finish his preparations, she sat on the gold pillow and immediately wished she had changed out of her suit. Slacks might not have given her the "don't touch" look she'd hoped to achieve, but they also wouldn't now be revealing an indecent amount of thigh.

If Eric noticed her skirt hiking up her legs, he said nothing. Lifting the pitcher, he held it above her small teacup. "Sake? I prefer mine warm. If, however, you prefer yours over ice . . ."

"No, this is fine," she said, though she had no idea which she preferred and had a feeling she should skip the sake altogether.

On the other hand the teacups were no bigger than a shot glass. A small amount of rice wine, she decided, certainly wasn't going to hurt her. It might even help her relax.

He poured the clear liquid into her cup, then into his. Lifting his with both hands, he waited for her to do the same. "*Kampai*," he said, his dark gaze locked on her face. "Cheers."

He downed the liquid in one gulp.

"*Kampai*," she repeated, boldly holding his gaze and following his example.

The liquid was warm as it slid down her throat and reminded her of sherry. It wasn't a bad taste, she decided. Not bad at all.

He refilled their cups, then placed a selection of the seafood, vegetables, and other ingredients from the casserole into their bowls before ladling in the broth. When he sat back and picked up his bowl with both hands to drink from it, she followed suit.

To her surprise the broth was delicious. "My compliments to the chef."

"The chef thanks you." Eric sipped his sake and wondered how he was going to get Ashley to let down her guard. She'd made it clear from the moment she'd stepped into his apartment that it was to be hands off tonight. He would honor her decision, but he did want to get beyond the surface of the woman, discover, if he might, what it was about her that he found so fascinating.

"Tell me about your family," he said.

"There's not much to tell."

He might have believed her if she hadn't tensed at his question, then downed her sake in one gulp. He poured more. "They live around here?"

"No. In Gary, Indiana." She gave a small smile. "Where they've lived all of their lives. My father works at a factory. My mother's health isn't the best, so she doesn't work."

"And your brother?"

He saw her take in a quick breath, the tension in her body even more discernible. "My brother's dead. What about your family?"

She was changing the subject. Eric let her. "Just my mother, my father, and me." He smiled. "I was such a hellion, they decided one was enough."

"You a hellion?" She drank down her sake. "Really?"

"That is what they tell me. Also, with my father traveling back and forth between Japan and the States, they decided one child was enough."

"Did your father meet your mother while he was in Japan?"

Eric nodded and poured more sake into her cup. "She was the daughter of one of the businessmen my father was dealing with at the time. I guess, from what they both say, it was love at first sight."

"That sounds romantic."

He'd always thought so, though he'd never truly believed in love at first sight. Not until the night he'd opened his door and seen Ashley standing in the hallway.

He did know that loving someone didn't mean life would go smoothly. "My mother gave up a great deal when she married my father."

"How's that?"

"She was from an upper-class Japanese family.

There were expectations for her. When she rebelled against her family and married my father, she was ostracized."

"That must have been rough on her."

He nodded. "It was. Her family still will not talk to her. As far as they are concerned, she is dead."

"And were you ostracized?"

"By her family?" He nodded. "To them, I do not exist."

"And by others?"

"Some," he admitted, then shrugged and took a sip of sake. "Quite a bit, actually. You see, I am neither fish nor fowl."

"You're a panther," she said.

"A panther?"

"A black panther." She also sipped from her cup, her gaze sliding down the front of him as she did. When she set her cup down, her smile made him wish he could read her mind. Reaching over, he poured more sake for her.

"Are you trying to get me drunk?"

"Maybe," he said, though he could also point out that in Japan it was considered good manners for the host to keep his guest's sake cup filled. If she didn't want any more, she should simply stop drinking.

She shook her head. "That's not playing fair."

"Ah, but you have heard, all is fair in love and war."

"And is this war?"

"I hope not."

"Love?"

He could see the quickening of her breathing the

moment she said the word, and he knew her heart had to be racing as fast as his. Softly, he answered, "Would it be so terrible if it was love, Ashley-san?"

The look of awareness in her eyes made him hold his breath, but when she stared down at her bowl of soup, she shook her head. "I can't fall in love . . . not now."

"Why not?"

"I'm going to Chicago."

"You got the transfer?"

"No, not yet." She looked up. "But I will. I have to."

"Have to?" he asked, surprised by her choice of words.

"I mean, it's been my plan for years. And now I'm so close."

"And there is no changing your plan?"

She hesitated, and he knew there was something she wasn't telling him. Finally, she sighed and shook her head. "I can't."

"Why, Ashley?"

"Because . . ." This time she was more determined. "Just because I can't."

"It is a law that you must do this?"

"No, of course not. Can't we talk about something else?"

"Like?"

"Like why are you a ninja?"

"Why do you not want to talk about going to Chicago?"

She ignored him. "Is your father a ninja?"

He wanted answers to his questions but decided

to give in to her. Patience was one thing a ninja knew well. And persistence.

With a laugh he answered her. "No, my father is not a ninja. He does know a little self-defense, and when I was a teenager, he was the one who paid for me to take karate lessons. But all he had in mind was for me to learn how to protect myself if necessary. He never thought I would become a ninja, take on *nin-po* as a way of life."

"He doesn't approve of your being a ninja?"

"He would be happier if I were using my degree and working for big business, but I would not say he disapproves of my being a ninja. It is just difficult for him to comprehend my lack of interest in making money."

"I find that difficult to comprehend too," Ashley admitted. From as early as she could remember, her father had stressed the importance of making money.

Locked into a job that sucked the energy and life from him, he'd pushed his son and daughter to do better. Ashley knew her brother would have made it.

If it hadn't been for her.

Quickly, she brought her thoughts back to Eric. "So how did you go from taking karate to becoming a ninja?"

"I met a man while I was in college. He was a guest lecturer, talking about the ninja myth. After I heard him, I told him my dissatisfaction with the karate I had learned.

"We talked for a long time, and I discovered that even though he lived in the States, he had been studying ninjutsu for years with a grand master in Japan.

He suggested that the next time I was in Japan, I go see the grand master. I did. It took only one visit, and I was hooked."

"And bam . . ." She snapped her fingers. "You were a ninja."

He chuckled and also snapped his fingers. "Bam and sixteen years later. Sixteen years of intensive study. What do you do for fun, Ashley?"

His question caught her off guard. "Fun?" She thought for a moment, stirring the shellfish around in her bowl with her fork. "I don't know. Sometimes, when I have time, I read a book . . . go to a movie."

"And do you date? Go out with men?"

"Nosy." She laughed self-consciously.

"I never hear any men come to your apartment."

"Maybe I go to their's."

He shook his head. "I do not think so. Have you ever had a lover?"

"Now you're getting personal."

"This dinner is to get to know each other. How else can I learn about you if I do not ask?" He paused. "I will tell you that I have slept with several women. But that was when I was young, when I felt I had to prove I was a man. Before I understood that manhood and being a man have nothing to do with sex."

The way he was looking at her, deep into her eyes, she knew he expected her to be as forthright. Uneasily, she shifted her position on her pillow and chewed on her lower lip. "Well, I've only slept with two men," she finally said. "And I guess if I was trying to prove anything, it was that I could do it."

"That you could do it," he repeated. "And did you love these two men?"

"I liked them. We were friends." She shrugged. "I'm not much of a romantic."

"Ah, but you have fire in your blood, Ashley-san," he said softly, his gaze never wavering.

"I have ambition," she countered, not liking the heat she felt running through her arteries at the moment.

"Passion."

"A goal."

He smiled. "You are afraid of what you feel when you are around me."

"I am not." She hoped she sounded positive, that he couldn't tell she was shaking inside. "I'm simply a realist. Why get involved with someone when there is no future for the relationship?"

"So we should ignore what we feel and go our separate ways? Is that it?"

That would be safest for her. She nodded, then looked down at the table. "I should be going. It's getting late."

"Very late," he said, but somehow she didn't think he was talking about the hour.

"Well, thank you for dinner." She rose awkwardly from the pillow, quickly pulling her skirt down. "It was delicious."

He glanced at her bowl, its contents barely touched, then he also rose to his feet. "I am glad you came."

He walked with her to the door, staying close enough that she could feel his presence with every step she took, but not once touching her. He watched her, saying nothing, as she slipped her high heels back on.

He still hadn't said anything when she reached for the doorknob, turning it but not pulling the door open. Standing there, she looked at him, at his thick dark hair; at his near-black almond-shaped eyes, which saw far too much for her comfort; and at his mouth, which she knew was firm and exciting and oh-so-arousing. She looked and knew she would spend the rest of the night wishing she'd had the nerve to discover why this man excited her so. Would spend the rest of her life wondering what she had missed.

"Ashley?"

At the sound of her name, she caught her breath, her gaze locked with his.

"Stay," he said softly. "Stay with me tonight."

She opened her mouth to say she couldn't, but somehow the words wouldn't come out. Promises made and a need to make up for what her selfishness had destroyed suddenly seemed very hazy. A stronger need, to love and be loved, ruled her thinking. Eric wanted her to stay, and she wanted to stay, to kiss that mouth that she knew would awaken the woman within, to be touched by his hands. She wanted to stay and make love with him the whole night through.

Slowly, she let go of the doorknob and kicked off her heels.

EIGHT

Eric touched the sleeve of her jacket, and Ashley took a step forward, holding her breath as butterflies skittered about in her stomach. She stared at his mouth—waiting with anticipation for the moment when his lips would touch hers.

She didn't have to wait long. His kiss was hungry and untamed, controlled yet totally unconstrained, sweeping her along with its wild passion, carrying her beyond reason to a realm of pure feeling and reaction. He kissed her, and he touched her, his hands skimming over her shoulders, down her spine to her bottom. He pressed his palms against the back of her skirt, bringing her hips against his so she could feel the hard evidence of his desire.

"You are yin and I am yang," he said raggedly, his words barely more than a whisper. "Opposites that attract and fulfill."

She had to admit, the attraction had been there from the first, growing each time they met, becoming more intense. Now she wanted him filling her, bringing relief to the ache deep within her. "Eric . . ."

She groaned his name, holding on to him for some form of stability. Her world was spinning, everything she'd so carefully set her sights on suddenly out of kilter. Never had she wanted to be touched and loved by a man as she did at this moment. Never had she felt the fire burning within her that now threatened to consume her.

His kisses fanned the flame as his hands moved to her hair, loosening the pins that held it back, freeing it as he freed her soul. She hesitated when he took a step backward, drawing her with him. Then she went willingly, following his lead, giving herself without reservation.

By the time he'd taken them to the middle of the room, he had her jacket off and had dropped it onto the carpeting. And by the time they were at the doorway to his bedroom, he was working on the buttons of her blouse.

He stopped backing up, his kisses interrupted as he concentrated on the buttons of her cuffs. He smiled when he succeeded in freeing them, then pulled her blouse from her skirt. The blouse, too, was dropped to the floor, and his gaze skimmed over the lace-trimmed nylon slip that covered her from above her breasts to her waist, then disappeared beneath her skirt. "You wear too many clothes, Ashley-san."

"But somehow I seem to be losing them."

He smiled broadly. "Somehow."

Her skirt went next, slipping from her hips to the carpet. She stepped out of it as Eric led her toward the futon on the floor of his bedroom.

His furnishings were sparse, the lighting dim. Sometime during their supper the music he'd had on had ended, and the only sounds now were the occasional faint slush of a car passing through the snow on the street below, and their ragged breathing. "I have dreamed of this moment," he said, brushing his fingertips over her cheek.

She glanced down at his simple Japanese bed and knew her dreams had never taken her this far. Even in her subconscious, she hadn't allowed herself to go beyond the pleasure of being held by him, kissed by him. The enormity of what she was about to do brought her gaze back to his face, and she suspected he could read her thoughts.

"I will take care of everything," he promised. "There will be no accidents, no danger to your future plans."

"I'm not very good at this," she confessed.

"There is no good or bad." Eric trailed his fingertips along the side of her face, letting them travel into her hair. "Only feelings."

She was so beautiful, she took his breath away, and he could not believe she had really agreed to stay. He wanted to tear her clothes from her, take her down on to his futon, and like the jungle cat she said he resembled, claim her as his own. Yet he knew he must go slowly. This was a moment to be appreciated, to be savored. And this was a woman who deserved to be pleasured.

He let his fingers slide over the velvet softness of her shoulder and down her arm, and he felt her shiver. "Cold?"

"No," she answered hoarsely, staring into his eyes.

"Good." His gaze dropped to her slip, and he knew it had to go next.

She did not stop him as he pulled it over her head, but she did put her hands on his arms when he reached to unclasp her bra. "You have too many clothes on," she said.

"Undress me," he answered, and waited to see what she would do.

Her hands seemed to tremble as she pulled his turtleneck from the waist of his jeans, and she chewed on her lower lip as she inched it up over his chest. He lifted his arms for her, bending his knees so she could pull it over his head.

The process brought her closer to his body. With her arms stretching upward, her bra touched his skin, its silky smoothness heated from within, the hard nubs of her nipples igniting a fire within him. He caught her hands, his shirt dangling between them above their heads. Then he had her hands behind her back, the shirt a common bond. A gentle exertion of pressure, and the entire length of her body was pressed against his.

He kissed her then, his tongue delving deep into her mouth and continuing the union, while the pressure of his need to take the union further became painfully uncomfortable within the confinement of his jeans. His shirt was discarded on the floor, and he reached for the snap of his jeans, not once relinquishing his hold on her mouth.

Her fingers found the snap before his. She released it, then hesitated. "Do it," he pleaded against her lips. "Please."

Cautiously, she pulled his zipper down, keeping it away from his body. He silently thanked her for her concern, then thrilled as her fingers brushed against his briefs and the hardness of his body, bringing him added pleasure.

She hesitated again, and he stepped back to pull off his jeans. She was smiling when he straightened to face her. "Do you always wear black?" she asked, her gaze on his black briefs, the rigid bulge in front clearly defined.

"It has become like a signature." He traced the frilly edge of her bra with a fingertip.

"The sign of the panther," she murmured, her hands going to his shoulders. With a sigh she gazed into his eyes. "Sometimes you frighten me, Eric."

"Do I frighten you now?" He brushed his knuckles over the front of her bra, teasing her nipples.

"Yes . . . no." Her breathing was shallow. "Now what you're doing is driving me crazy."

He knew they were driving each other crazy and that there was only one way to sanity. He released the clasp of her bra, freeing her breasts, then cupped them in his hands. Bending down, he pressed adoring kisses on each. "So perfect," he said, his words taking in all of her.

She licked her lips, and a tremor ran the length of her body. "Not perfect," she said shyly. "The other times . . . When I've made love . . . I've, ah . . ."

"You have what?" He straightened and drew her close, wrapping his arms around her. "What happened, Ashley? What are you afraid of?"

"Nothing happened," she confessed, avoiding his gaze. "I mean, they seemed satisfied, but . . ."

She didn't finish, yet he understood. "But it was *you* who were not satisfied." He forced her to look at him. "Tell me, Ashley-san, am I like the others?"

"No," Ashley said. Nothing about Eric was like any other man she had ever known, not even a simple kiss.

"And when I touch you, does it feel good?"

"Yes." Good. Wonderful. Exciting. Words couldn't describe how he made her feel, all warm and feminine.

"How good?" He slid his hands down her back to her bottom and slipped his fingers under the nylon of her panties.

She sucked in a breath. "Very good."

"Then will you trust me? Will you give up your worries and simply let our bodies and souls find their happiness?" He pressed her against his hardness, teasing her with a slow, rubbing motion of his hips, and good turned to wild and crazy.

He was arousing her to a fevered pitch of need, her skin growing hot, a moist warmth flowing between her legs. Breathing was becoming difficult; talk almost impossible. "Eric, stop," she groaned.

"Because it does not feel good?"

"Because if feels too good."

He chuckled and pulled back the thick downy

comforter that covered his bed, then laid her down on the sheet-covered futon. In one fluid motion he slipped off her panties. His briefs went next, and for a moment he stood at the end of his bed, naked and proud, gazing down at her as she gazed up at him. Then he knelt over her, spreading her legs with his knees before bending close to feather kisses over her skin.

He licked and he nipped and he sucked, drawing her nipples, one by one, into his mouth. And as his mouth teased, his hands aroused her, his fingers traveling over her body—massaging, caressing, exciting.

It took her longer to get the nerve to touch him, even to run her hands over his shoulders and along the sides of his ribs. Every time she reached his hips, she moved her hands back up, until she knew by his frustrated groan that he wanted more.

When she did touch him between his legs, her fingers wrapping around the hard length of him, he suddenly tensed, and so did she. Immediately, she released her grip, only to have him catch her hand and bring it back. "Please," he begged.

She pleased and he teased, the play of his fingers exciting her more and more. When she was writhing beneath his touch and certain she could stand no more, he stopped and drew away from her, reaching into a drawer in the low nightstand by his futon.

He fumbled a bit as he opened the packet, and she was glad he wasn't an expert. She watched as he moved back over her, then she closed her eyes and waited for the thrusts and grunts she knew would come.

Only it was the flick of his tongue she felt. First

around and into her navel, then down her abdomen and along the soft inner skin of her thighs. She held her breath and waited as his teasing tongue moved higher, then she gasped and opened her eyes, staring down at the top of his head.

"Eric," she groaned, reaching out to stop him.

Her fingers became entwined in his hair, tightening against his scalp as the pleasure he was bringing overruled embarrassment. She held on as he carried her to a height beyond her dreams, to the edge of sanity, to the brink of ecstasy.

As she hovered there, he swiftly moved his body over hers, his kisses switching to her mouth, his knees driving her legs farther apart. He entered her, not with a thrust but slowly and patiently, giving her pleasure, not pain.

Only when she had accepted him did he begin to move, each stroke taking her on a journey, until she knew that this time would be nothing like the others, that the man inside of her was not merely finding his satisfaction but was making her complete.

She cried out when she went over the brink, her body shuddering, and she knew her life would never be the same. And as his thrusts increased in tempo, she was taken upward again, carried further than she thought possible, until she was certain she would die.

He gasped, crying out a word in Japanese, and she called to him, not caring what she said, only knowing that everything in the world was perfect, if only for that moment.

It was a while before he moved. He covered her with the comforter he'd earlier pushed aside, briefly left her to go into the bathroom, then turned off the light and got into bed beside her. She said nothing, too stunned to speak. Finally, he reached over and touched her arm. "Are you all right?"

"I'm fine," she lied, too confused by what had happened to know how she felt.

"Sorry you stayed?"

"No." That was the truth. She would never be sorry for what she'd just experienced.

He was quiet again. She thought he'd gone to sleep, then she heard him take in a deep breath and exhale. He turned on his side, facing her, and she could feel his gaze. Under the comforter he touched her, his hand warm as it grazed the side of one breast.

"Ashley," he said hesitantly. "Were you satisfied?"

"Yes," she whispered, still a little shocked by the experience. "More than satisfied."

"Good." His hand slid up to her face, and he traced the outline of her jaw to her cheek. "Strange," he said, his voice a soothing caress. "Just when I think I know something, I discover how little I do know."

She knew she'd discovered many things in the last few hours. She'd learned that she had no control when it came to Eric Newman, that his kisses awoke in her an insatiable need that only he could satisfy. And that even in her satisfaction, she wanted more.

When he pulled her closer, molding her body to his, she felt a new awareness awaken deep within her, a new craving that cried to be fulfilled. As he grew hard against her, she knew she was not alone in this hunger.

"Ashley?"

The way he said her name, she realized the need surprised him as much as it did her. Sliding her hand down between them, she stroked him and whispered his name.

Early the next morning Ashley opened her eyes. Faint light filtered into the bedroom through venetian blinds, and from the street below came the intermittent sounds of traffic. It took her a moment to remember it was Saturday and that she was not in her bed, but in Eric's. It took her only a second longer to realize he wasn't beside her.

She sat up, pulling the comforter to her shoulders to cover her nakedness. He was across the room, kneeling on a woven mat, his back to her. A black silk robe decorated across the back with the colorful pattern of a dragon was wrapped around his body and tucked under his knees. He sat straight and unmoving, his hands resting on his thighs.

She watched, waiting to see what he was doing, only to discover that he was doing nothing. He sat as he was without moving, without seeming to breathe, saying nothing. Then she sneezed. She saw his shoulders twitch and sensed that he took in a breath. Gracefully, he rose to his feet and turned to face her, his expression serene and relaxed.

"You were praying?" she asked.

"Meditating."

"You do that every morning?" She'd been told it was beneficial . . . told by co-workers who were trying to be helpful and who thought she needed to slow down and relax.

"I try to do it in the morning and at night."

She grinned. "I don't remember you doing it last night."

He tightened the belt around his robe and walked toward her. "I had something else on my mind last night."

"Oh, really?" She held her breath as he neared the bed, a giddy sensation playing in her stomach and lower.

"Really." He slipped under the comforter, the silk of his robe caressing her thigh, and his toes touching her ankle. His skin was cool, the feel intimate. Automatically, the muscles between her legs tightened.

She couldn't believe it. They'd made love most of the night. She couldn't possibly want more.

Yet when he leaned close and kissed her, she knew she did. As his hands swept over her body, arousing her in ways she'd never known before meeting him, the need once again begged to be satisfied.

It was much later in the morning when Ashley again opened her eyes. The room was lighter, and the needs she now felt were for a bathroom and food.

Eric lay beside her, sleeping peacefully, his breathing deep and regular. Slowly and carefully, she slipped out from under the arm draped across her hips and inched her way to the edge of the futon. She moved as quietly as she could, not wanting to wake him, and tiptoed to his bathroom. The muscles of her inner thighs complained with every step she took.

In the bathroom she stared at the woman looking back at her from the vanity mirror. The face she saw was familiar, yet completely strange. Her hair was mussed from hours of making love, her lips swollen from endless kisses, and the circles under her eyes attested to how little sleep she'd gotten.

"What have you done?" she asked her image.

"Spent the night with a man," she answered for herself.

It wasn't the first time, though she had to admit, this was the first time she'd ever felt so satisfied the next morning. So . . .

Happy, she realized, and grinned.

"What you did," she told herself, "was find out that you could enjoy sex."

That wasn't exactly a terrible thing for a woman of twenty-seven to discover. Not a bad thing at all, she decided as she took a hot shower. No need to worry that making love with Eric would change her life.

It couldn't.

To let it do so would be to let her father down. Break her promise to her brother.

By the time she'd dried her body and had managed to give her hair some semblance of order, she was sure she had everything in perspective. She'd made love with a man who turned her on, and she had thoroughly enjoyed the experience. Making love, though, didn't necessarily have anything to do with being in love, and what she'd done in no way changed her plans for the future.

No way at all.

Still, she wasn't quite ready to face Eric. Rather than go back into the bedroom for her clothes, she simply wrapped one of his large white towels around her body and tucked it into itself above her breasts.

As she headed for his kitchen, she did pick up her blouse and jacket from the floor, placing them on a stool by the counter. Then she began looking for something to eat.

The seafood casserole from the night before was still sitting on the table where they'd left it. It looked totally unappetizing, and she carried it back into the kitchen and left it beside the sink. She also took care of the earthenware pitcher of sake, their cups, their bowls of barely eaten food, and the utensils.

She was staring into the refrigerator when she felt a tug on the back of her towel. The ends pulled loose, and the material began to fall away from her body. She squealed and grabbed for it.

Holding the ends together, she turned to face Eric. "Don't sneak up on a person like that. You could give someone a heart attack."

"I am sorry." He grinned and helped her secure the towel. "I did not mean to scare you."

"Oh, yeah?" She ran her fingertips over the front of his silk robe. "Then make some noise when you walk."

Chuckling, he leaned close and brushed her mouth with a kiss. "Here I spend years learning how to move without making a sound, and now you want me to make noise. Good morning. What were you looking for?"

Remembering, she turned back to the refrigerator. "Food. What do you eat for breakfast?"

He also looked. "I have fruit and eggs."

"No frozen muffins? No sweet rolls?"

"Muffins are high in fat," he said, pulling out a carton of eggs. "Sweet rolls—"

"I know. High in sugar." She watched him set the eggs on the counter. "But those things are high in cholesterol."

And she really didn't like eggs.

"An occasional egg will not harm you, especially if you exercise regularly."

She wasn't about to tell him she never exercised, unless running up and down the stairs to her apartment counted. Or what they'd done the night before. "I think I'll just get dressed and see what I have at my place."

He was already breaking eggs into a bowl. "I'll have breakfast ready before you're dressed."

"You don't need to," she said, but he continued breaking eggs, so she decided not to argue.

And he was right. Even though she didn't put all of her clothes back on—just her panties, skirt, and blouse—when she walked back into the kitchen, he had two plates on the counter, each with a mound of eggs nestled on a spinach leaf and surrounded by decorative slices of apple.

"How does this look?" he asked, and she knew she couldn't leave without at least pretending to eat a little.

"Looks nutritious," she said, scooting up on a stool.

Her first bite was cautious, her second a little more enthusiastic. To her surprise the eggs actually tasted good. "Hey, this isn't bad. Not bad at all. Different."

"My mother often fixed eggs this way."

"You are a good cook." She laughed and went back to her eggs. "I never learned that domestic skill, so I usually end up ruining anything I try to make from scratch. Safest thing, I've found, is to eat out, have the food delivered, or stick to things I can pop in the microwave or toaster."

"Your mother never taught you to cook?" Eric found that surprising. His had insisted he learn.

"That's a laugh," she said, but he noticed she didn't laugh.

"Your mother did not like to cook?"

"My mother . . ." she started, then frowned. "Is this another of your inquisitions?"

"I am just trying to get to know you."

"I think you got to know me pretty well last night." Grinning, she put a hand on his leg and ran her fingers over his robe, up toward his hips.

He knew she was trying to change the subject, distract him, and the way his body was responding, it wasn't going to take much for her to succeed. He captured her hand in his, stopping its upward movement. "If you do not want to talk about your mother, tell me about your father."

She eyed him suspiciously. "What do you want to know about my father?"

"You have a good relationship with him?"

"Yes."

"What is he like?" Eric had a feeling it was important he know.

"A hard worker. A man with unfulfilled dreams."

"What kind of dreams?"

"Dreams of being a success, of getting out of the factory. Only nothing ever worked out right for him." Her sigh was barely audible. "Not even his dream for Jack."

"Your brother?"

"Yes."

"The one who died?"

She nodded, but through her hand he could feel her tension. Gently, he caressed her fingers. "You were how old when your brother died?"

"Ten. I was ten, and Jack was eighteen."

"That is quite a difference in ages."

She looked up. "I was an accident. My mother had had her tubes clipped. Or so they thought. Either the doctor did a sloppy job or one grew back together."

"You must have been quite a surprise."

"More than a surprise." Pulling her hand free from his grasp, Ashley slid off her stool and picked up her plate. "You want to know about my mother. Well, I'll tell you about my mother. She would have been a lot better off if I'd never been born."

NINE

Eric tried to keep his expression bland, but the bitterness in Ashley's voice both pained and startled him. Still, he did not think she was looking for sympathy. "Why do you say that?" he asked. "That you shouldn't have been born."

"Because I drove her over the edge."

Ashley carried her plate to the sink, then turned and looked back at him. He watched her closely. Her eyes had lost their sparkle, and her voice was tense. Even her coloring seemed faded, washed out.

"The reason the doctor tied my mother's tubes," she said, "was she was prone to periods of depression. She really loved my brother and took good care of him, but the doctors felt that more than one baby would be too much for her. And they were right. When I was born, she went into a deep depression. All of my life she's been in and out of hospitals."

He wanted to tell her it wasn't her fault and that he was glad she'd been born. He wanted to go to her and hold her tight, to take away the pain he saw in her eyes, but he forced himself to stay on his stool and continue probing. Understanding this about Ashley was essential. "That must have been rough on you."

"It has been," she said.

"And what about your father? How has he treated you?"

"My father's had a rough life," she said slowly. "He's tried to be a good parent, make up for Mom's illness, but it hasn't been easy. Actually, when I was growing up, I saw very little of him. He was always working, putting in as much overtime as he could. He had to, to pay the medical bills."

"You did not have insurance?"

"Oh, we had it. Keeping that insurance was one reason Dad could never do what he really wanted, quit his job and move to Chicago. But even good medical insurance doesn't pay all of the bills. And believe me, my mother runs up the bills."

"So you did not see much of your father when you were growing up." Eric was beginning to get a picture of her childhood. A mentally ill mother. An overworked father. "What was your brother like?"

She smiled, walking back toward him. "My brother was wonderful. The best. And he was really smart. I remember him sitting me down and talking to me just like I was all grown up. He used to point out ways spokespeople for the government and businesses would slant information in their reports so they'd get what they wanted. I know it was listening to him that got me interested in public relations."

Stopping in front of Eric, she grinned. "You know, you'd be a good PR man. You're an expert at getting people to do what you want."

"Such as?" He rubbed his palms over the sleeves of her blouse.

"Such as getting me to spend the night with you and tell you about my family. Not too many people know about my mother. It's not something I like to talk about."

"Then what you have said is between you and me."

"Ninja's honor?" she asked, lifting her right hand.

"Ninja's honor," he promised, raising his. Before she could move away, he caught her hand and drew her closer. "And have I convinced you to learn self-defense?"

"I need to learn some kind of defense . . . from you."

"I am not the enemy, Ashley."

Maybe not the enemy, she thought, but he was a threat—an emotional danger. "What do you want from me, Eric?"

"Nothing you are not ready to give."

"I'm still the same person I was yesterday." Yet even as she said it, she knew it wasn't true. Spending the night with Eric had changed her.

"I like that person," he said softly.

"That person is going to Chicago."

"I understand."

She hoped he did. "So this relationship we have, we're just . . . ?"

"Friends. Lovers." He smiled. "Friendly lovers. We see each other when we can, make no demands on each other, and do not ask the other to change."

"Friendly lovers," she repeated. It might work, and it would certainly make living next door to Eric a lot easier. No more berating herself for wanting what she could not have; no more frustrated nights filled with erotic dreams.

Grinning, she leaned closer. "Sounds good to me, friend."

All day Tuesday Eric felt restless and on edge. Ashley had said she would attend class that night if nothing came up at work. On Monday he'd brought her a gi and taught her how to tie her belt around the uniform. He'd also told her she was going to have to cut her fingernails.

She'd said she'd have to think about that, and when he'd left her apartment early that morning, she still hadn't cut them.

He really had no idea if she'd come at all.

His youth classes seemed to drag by, and as seven o'clock drew closer, he found himself tensing every time the outside door opened and someone came in. It wasn't until he saw her, standing hesitantly in the doorway, that he breathed a sigh of relief.

She had come.

Now all he had to do was pretend she was just another student.

The moment she smiled at him, he knew that wasn't going to be easy. And when she walked out of the women's dressing room, he knew he'd never seen anyone look sexier in a gi.

Or more nervous.

She'd taken her hair out of its usual twist and pulled it back into a ponytail, and under her jacket, she wore a pink T-shirt. Without her usual tailored suit and hairstyle and the earrings, rings, and bracelets she always wore, she looked younger. Less sophisticated.

She glanced around the room, her gaze at last coming to rest on him. He nodded, hoping his smile gave her the confidence she needed without revealing their relationship.

He'd told her what to expect during class, beginning with the opening ritualistic bows and words. He waited to introduce her to the other students until after the warm-up session.

As Eric introduced her, Ashley nodded and smiled at the students around her. The way he made the announcement, it sounded as though she were simply a woman who had stepped into his dojo and asked to learn how to defend herself. She doubted anyone there would guess she was the sensei's lover.

She'd spent the day worrying about how she would act, and if she was making a mistake. Most of all, she hoped she wasn't so out of shape that she'd make a total fool of herself.

To her surprise some of the exercises she'd learned as a child taking gymnastics were part of the warm-up Eric led them through. And when they began working on a specific maneuver, everyone was helpful. If she didn't catch on immediately, her partner or someone else would help. It seemed to be the rule that the more skilled worked with the less able.

Not too long into the class, a good-looking blond man with a green belt wrapped around his jacket appointed himself her caretaker. Several times that evening he offered his assistance. Before the next class began on Thursday night, he formally introduced himself. "My name's Dan Turner," he said, extending his hand and smiling warmly. "I was really impressed by how quickly you caught on Tuesday night."

"Thank you." She shook his hand, thrilled that he thought she'd done well. Eric had praised her, but she'd known he would. He wanted her taking the class.

"If you need any extra help tonight," Dan went on, "just let me know."

"I probably will." Her fear was she wouldn't remember *anything* she'd learned on Tuesday.

Glancing around, she noticed Eric watching them.

Suddenly realizing Dan was still holding her hand, she pulled hers free.

At first, when Dan kept coming over to help her—whether she needed it or not—she wondered if Eric had asked him to keep an eye on her. But halfway through the drill and practice time, she began to suspect Dan was initiating the contact on his own. Every time she turned around, he was by her side. And every time she looked at Eric, he was staring at her, his expression unreadable but his gaze intense.

Concentrating on what she was supposed to be learning was becoming difficult. She'd been paired with a woman about her size, and two out of the four times Kathy grabbed her, Ashley managed to break free. Maybe not the way they'd been shown, but she was free.

After the fourth time she saw, to her dismay, Dan once again walking toward her, this time shaking his head. "No, no, no," he said. "Not like that."

Nudging her partner aside, he stepped behind Ashley. "Maybe that works with someone Kathy's size, but what if I grabbed you like this?"

His arms snaked around her, trapping her like a vise, and he pulled her back snug against his body. "What would you do now?" he asked, his cheek flush with hers, the stubble of his beard rubbing her skin.

Ashley felt a moment of panic. Dan was holding her too close, his arms intimately wrapped around her so they pressed against her breasts. She was trapped, truly trapped, and the situation seemed too real, the sound of his breathing too irregular. Automatically, she looked across the mat for Eric.

As she'd expected, he was watching.

He started toward them, and she breathed a sigh of relief. He would tell Dan to ease up, take it easy on her.

Only it wasn't Dan he spoke to.

"Okay, how are you going to get out of that?" Eric asked, stopping a few feet away.

"You tell me," she said, irritated that he wasn't responding with at least a little more concern.

"What are you supposed to do?"

She tried to remember. She also tried twisting, as she had with Kathy. Twisting didn't work. Dan simply tightened his grip, holding her even closer.

"Stop," Eric said sternly. "And this time listen."

"I did listen," she said, but she knew she hadn't. Somewhere between when Eric had started his demonstration and ended it, her mind had drifted to what they'd done the night before. She didn't think she should mention that.

"Center yourself," he ordered. "Give a yell, crouch low, and throw him off balance."

She remembered that much. Trying to think of a point two inches below her belly, she yelled and crouched as he'd shown.

She thought she did pretty well, even though she didn't completely free herself. Eric made her do it again. And again, dropping down farther and harder each time.

"Now an elbow jab back to his stomach."

She was getting tired of Dan's arms around her, and she jabbed. Eric made her change the position of her arm and jab again.

"Now, a fist to his groin."

"If you say so," she grumbled, and she had a feeling Dan could sense her growing anger. He protected his groin.

Still, Eric made her repeat the move.

He made her repeat every step of the exercise, ending with a kick to Dan's knee and a twist of his wrist that put Dan on the mat, his knee supposedly dislocated and his arm broken.

"There," she said with satisfaction, wiping her hands together as she stepped away from Dan's supine body and toward Eric. She'd finally made it through the damn exercise, and she'd done it well, even if she did say so herself.

"Now do it again," Eric said without a smile. "All the way from the start."

"Again?" she gasped, and glanced back at Dan. He was rising from the mat, grinning like a schoolboy.

"Again," Eric ordered.

So she did it again. And again, and again. By the time Eric nodded and gave his okay, she was sure she could execute the routine in her sleep. She was also ready to drop, every muscle in her body protesting. Sighing, she watched Eric walk away.

Dan heard her and chuckled. Slipping an arm around her shoulders, he gave her a hug. "He's a taskmaster, isn't he? But you did a good job."

She grunted, grateful that someone thought so. Eric certainly hadn't seemed pleased.

Later, as she and the others knelt on the mat and watched Eric and a brown-belt student work out, Ashley wondered what she had wanted from him. A big hug? A gold star?

"I will not give you special treatment," he'd told her before she even started. "It will be as though you are just another student."

She'd said she understood, but had she?

She hated to admit it, but she did want more from him—the hug at least. Perhaps because she'd gotten so few hugs in her life, at least from the people who counted. Perhaps because she wanted everyone at his dojo to know that she was someone special in Eric's life.

She wanted to be able to say, "I know this man better than any of you."

Only she wondered if she did.

One thing she had learned—Dan was right: Eric was a taskmaster. She would never forget how to escape an attack from the rear. But watching Eric execute the same escape, every movement of his body a lesson in grace, she knew she had a lot more to learn.

"He's amazing, isn't he?" Dan whispered, kneeling beside her.

She nodded, then jerked her head his way. Dan had covered her hand with his.

Unsure of what to do or say, she looked down at the mat where Dan's fingers touched hers, then up at Eric.

He had stopped what he was doing and was staring at her . . . at them. Still, she was sure he was aware of the student he was working with coming up behind him, was certain Eric would amaze her as usual and move just as the man made his attack.

Only he didn't.

With a yell the student grabbed Eric, and Eric's feet left the mat.

His mouth opened with surprise . . . then he hit the mat.

For a moment there was silence, then Eric rose and Dan chuckled softly. "I have never seen anyone catch the sensei off guard," he murmured. "Something must have distracted him."

"Must have," Ashley agreed, pulling her hand away from Dan's. She had a feeling she knew exactly what had distracted Eric.

As soon as class was over, she started toward him,

but Dan stopped her by catching her hand. "Have time to go out for a coffee?"

"Coffee?"

"There's a restaurant just down the road."

She knew then that she needed to cool Dan's interest. Pulling her hand free from his and shaking her head, she tried to be subtle. "Sorry, but I've got to head straight home. I've got clothes to wash."

"Maybe tomorrow night, then?" he suggested. "Maybe we could go out to dinner?"

Since subtle hadn't worked, she decided to be blunt. "Dan, I already have a boyfriend."

"Oh." For a moment he looked crestfallen, then he shrugged. "Well, if you and he ever break up . . ."

She certainly wouldn't call him. She said nothing, though, merely smiled and nodded. As Dan walked away, she glanced around the room for Eric.

He was nowhere to be seen.

She didn't see him again until she was back in her street clothes. By that time he'd already started his advanced class, and she knew she would have to wait until he got home before they could talk about what had happened.

She'd planned on doing her laundry right away, but she'd underestimated how tired she was. Once inside her apartment, she made it to her couch and no farther. Closing her eyes, she told herself she'd just rest a moment. The next sound she heard was a loud knock on her door.

Startled, she jumped, her heart lodged somewhere in her throat. Confused and barely able to speak, she called out, "Who is it?"

The answer was clear and sharp. "Eric."

After taking a moment to chase the fog from her mind, she rose and walked across the room to the door. Still, when she opened her door, she felt groggy. "Hi," she said sleepily. "Long time no see."

Eric snorted and looked beyond her, into her apartment. "I was not sure you would even be here."

His eyes were cold, his tone frigid, and she was suddenly wide awake. "Why do you say that?"

"I thought you would be out with Dan. Or is he here?"

"No." That he even thought Dan might be upset her. "Last I saw of him was at the dojo."

"Well, he left right after you did." Eric scowled. "Right after you and he had your little tête-à-tête."

She lifted her chin and looked him straight in the eyes. "Tête-à-tête?"

"Do you deny you have been flirting with him?"

"Yes, I deny it. I have not been flirting with anyone!"

"Is that so? And what do you call holding hands with a man when you should be watching a demonstration? Holding hands after class?"

"I'd call it poor eyesight on your part. I was not holding hands with Dan during that demonstration. He put his hand over mine. And after class he grabbed my hand."

Eric bowed slightly, as though her confession had confirmed his argument.

"Don't go bowing to me!" she snapped. "And don't go jumping to conclusions."

His expression turned hard. "Look, if you want to

hustle guys, that is your business, but not while you are at my dojo. I will not have you distracting my students. Not during class."

"I have not been hustling guys. It's your student who was hustling me. And I'm sorry if you were distracted, but it wasn't by my doing."

Once again, he scoffed. "And while we are at it, your nails are too long."

She held up her hands and looked at her nails. Never in her life had they been as short as they were now. "They are not."

"Yes, they are," he growled, his eyes narrowing. "If you plan on attending any more classes, cut them."

He turned and walked toward his apartment. She wasn't about to leave it at that. "Eric Newman, come back here!"

He stopped where he was and faced her, but he didn't come back.

He didn't say a word, either, so she went on. "You listen to me. I have not been flirting with your students, I am not interested in flirting with your students, and if they or you are distracted, that's your problem, not mine."

She started to slam her door shut, then stopped herself, jerking it open again. "And my nails are not too long!"

Then she did slam her door.

A moment later she heard him slam his door.

Let him, she decided. If he wanted to act like an idiot, fine. How dare he accuse her of flirting with other men!

Here she'd thought he was different—exciting,

mysterious. Perfect. What he was, was a blind, ignorant fool.

She went into her bathroom and pulled every piece of dirty laundry from her hamper, tossing it into her laundry basket. Then she grabbed her wash money, detergent, and keys and headed for the basement.

Still fuming, she sorted her clothes and applied spot remover to any spots she found. "Idiot!" she said over and over, not sure if she meant Eric or herself.

That she even cared what he thought bothered her. She'd been right from the start. Getting involved with a man was a mistake. What had she been thinking? She'd promised herself she would make things up to her father, be the success he always wanted. Well, this certainly wasn't the way. Here she was, emotionally and physically drained and on the verge of tears.

No, this wasn't the way at all.

As the two washers filled with water, she leaned back against one and closed her eyes, trying to relax. In the solitude of the basement she listened to the flow of the water, to the clicks and hisses of the furnace, and to the thud of her heart.

Then she heard the faintest creak, and her eyes snapped open.

Eric stood on the stairway, halfway down.

For a moment she could only stare at him, knowing that no matter how much he upset her, he would always seem mysterious and exciting. And thinking he was an idiot didn't stop her heart from racing or her mouth from going completely dry.

"I just started them," she said, even though he

wasn't carrying any dirty clothes. "It will be a while before there's an empty washer."

"I do not need a washer." Slowly, he continued on down the stairs.

She watched him near and held her breath.

An arm's length away, he stopped. "I came down to apologize."

She was tempted to say something but didn't. In silence she studied his face and waited for him to go on.

"It, ah . . . bothers me to have to say this."

He paused, but she still said nothing.

"I, ah . . ." He inhaled deeply, then exhaled and went on. "I think I am the one with a problem. I think I have been jealous."

"But there's no reason to be," she finally said. "How could I be interested in any other man with you around?"

"He is good-looking."

"Blue-eyed blonds are a dime a dozen." She gazed into his dark almond-shaped eyes. "I prefer a panther."

Stepping toward him, she touched his arm. "Eric, I never meant to do anything to make you jealous."

He glanced down at her hand and smiled ruefully. "Simply being yourself is enough. I am not surprised Dan finds you attractive. And I know we are only friends, but—"

Squeezing his arm, she stopped him. "Friends sometimes get jealous. And I'm sorry about Dan. It's just that everyone at your dojo is so friendly, I didn't realize he was coming on to me, not at first. I thought he was just being helpful, that you'd asked him to help me. If I did say or do something that gave him the wrong impression, I didn't mean to."

"It is my fault. I jumped to conclusions."

"Yes, you did," she agreed, and laughed. "And that could be dangerous. Look what happened when you thought Dan and I were holding hands during your demonstration."

Eric frowned. "What did happen?"

"You got thrown. Dan said it was the first time he's ever seen you caught off guard."

Eric chuckled, and she felt him relax. "With you, I am experiencing a lot of firsts. Forgive me?"

"You're forgiven." How could she not forgive him?

Wrapping her arms around his waist, she hugged him close and turned her face up to his. The washers spun, then filled again, but she didn't notice or care. All she cared about was being with Eric, tasting his kisses, and knowing the wedge that had come between them was gone.

Later, as she snuggled beside him on his futon, satisfied and content, she didn't even care that she'd be dead tired in the morning or that her clothes were still in the washers. Somehow, she was sure, everything would work out all right.

When Eric ran his fingertips over her breasts, though, she remembered the one thing they still had not settled. Catching his hand, she scratched his palm. "My nails are not too long."

His fingers clamped around hers. "Yes, they are."

Stubbornly, she persisted. "If I were a man, would you make me cut my nails shorter?"

"If you were a man, I would not want to be having this discussion right now." He chuckled, then turned serious. "Cut them."

TEN

Ashley cut her fingernails shorter. And she went to class Saturday and Tuesday, then drove to Indiana Wednesday night to be with her parents over the Thanksgiving weekend. Thursday night, though, she was back in Ann Arbor.

As she climbed the stairs to the second floor of the apartment building, she met Charlie coming down. "I thought you were spending Thanksgiving with your folks," he said, stopping on the step above her.

"I did." And all during the drive back to Ann Arbor, she'd wondered why.

"Well?" Charlie cocked his head, his eyebrows arching slightly. "What happened? Last I remember, you said you wouldn't be back until Sunday."

She couldn't tell him what had happened, not what really happened. Instead, she held up her briefcase. "I changed my mind. I have a lot of work to do."

"Gal, you work too much."

She sighed, remembering her conversation with her father. "It's more like I'm not working enough. I think, for a moment, I forgot where I'm going."

"And where are your going?" Charlie asked very seriously.

"To Chicago."

She was on track again. Had a plan. She'd get there either by transferring to Stedfeld's main office or by finding a job with some other company. Her father had made it clear that Jack wouldn't have wasted five years in a place like Ann Arbor, that he would have been in the big city by now, making a "real" name for himself.

"Chicago," Charlie repeated, wrinkling his nose and shaking his bald head. "Why you want to live and work there is beyond me. That place is almost as bad as Detroit for muggings and shootings."

"It's the hub of the Midwest." She couldn't count how often her father had said that. "Queen City of the Lakes."

"Windy City, that's what it is. But if you're looking for queens, I'm sure you'll find them there."

Ashley laughed, relaxing for the first time that day. "You know we'll never agree on this, Charlie. Maybe you don't like Chicago, but I was raised by a man who loves the city. I'm afraid you're battling too many years of hearing my father praise Chi Town, too many memories of visits to the zoo and aquarium, to museums and baseball games at Wrigley Field. When my brother was alive, every weekend my father didn't have to work, he'd take us there. I've grown up with the message that if you're not living and working in Chicago, you really haven't made it."

"And you buy that?"

"I buy it," she said firmly, knowing she did. Bought it, believed it, and felt compelled to fulfill it.

Charlie scoffed. "If Chicago's so great, why isn't your father working there?"

"He would be if he could." But because of her, he couldn't.

She couldn't change the fact that she'd been born, and she couldn't bring back her brother, but she could give the man who'd sacrificed so much a little happiness.

"Charlie?" a woman asked hesitantly from below them.

Ashley glanced down and saw an older woman standing on the first-floor landing. She was big-busted and slim-hipped, wearing a blue sweatshirt that was covered with glittery sequins and black stretch pants that disappeared into a pair of black boots. Her hair was a silvery blue, and her makeup was on the garish side, but she was a fairly attractive woman.

"Edie," Charlie said, then quickly corrected himself. "I mean Mrs. Wyconski. This is Ashley, the one whose purse you found. Mrs. Wyconski lives in the apartment building down the street. We play bingo together on Wednesday nights."

The way Edie Wyconski was looking at Charlie, Ashley had a feeling the two of them played more than just bingo together. Grabbing the opportunity to excuse herself, she did and hurried on past Charlie, up the stairs.

In her apartment she laid her briefcase on the breakfast bar and took her suitcase into the bedroom. There, she collapsed on her bed, exhausted.

What a day.

She hated holidays. They always brought back memories. It had been seventeen years, but she could still remember the last Thanksgiving she'd spent with her brother. Back then, Thanksgiving was a fun day, a family event, with aunts and uncles and cousins congregating at one house for the traditional meal.

Seventeen years ago, it had been at their house. Her mother was having a good day—her son was home from college, and Jack had been the center of everyone's attention. Over and over aunts and uncles asked how he liked college and what he was going to do after he graduated. He told them he planned to go into public relations, get a job at Stedfeld's because it was the largest public-relations firm in the Midwest, and live somewhere on Lake Shore Drive.

Ten-year-old Ashley listened and longed for the same attention.

She wasn't sure when she decided to follow Jack's path. All she knew was when her high school counselor asked her what her career plans were, she said she wanted to go into public relations. When she graduated from college, the first place she went to apply for a job was Stedfeld's.

During their dinner earlier that afternoon, her father had actually said that Jack would be proud of her . . . especially if she got the transfer to Chicago. Of course, that was before she said anything about taking lessons in self-defense.

Oh, how she wished she could go back in time. Back seventeen years. Back five hours.

This year, as every year since Jack's death, the three of them had gone out for Thanksgiving dinner. Not to someone's home—her father felt being around family and the memories would be too painful for her mother. No, they'd driven to a nearby hotel and sat at a table at the back of the restaurant, commenting on how many people ate out on Thanksgiving. Her father had ordered a cocktail and once again congratulated her on her promotion. And her mother had actually smiled at her.

It had almost been a cheerful occasion—until she started talking about what she was learning at Eric's dojo. She mentioned working out on a mat, and her mother started crying and carrying on.

A mat. Who would think such a simple statement would cause such trauma?

She tried to explain how learning martial arts was nothing like when she'd taken gymnastics lessons. But if her mother heard and understood, she didn't respond. Within minutes she was too upset for them to finish their meal.

Her mother's depression, Ashley knew from past experience, would last for days. She would weep and wail for the child she'd lost and curse the child she'd never wanted.

At first Ashley had offered to stay, for her father's sake. It became clear, though, that her staying would only make matters worse, so she'd packed her bag and headed back to Ann Arbor. The trip had allowed her time to think of her past and her future. Three-and-a-half hours on the road had given her a chance to evaluate goals and motives, guilt and obligations. She knew what she had to do . . . and why.

Clearly, from the first time she'd met Eric, all reason had escaped her. She couldn't explain why, but he'd become an obsession. A need. Being with him was taking on too much importance. She'd gone to class Tuesday night, then to his apartment, when she really should have stayed at the office and worked on a speech.

She was jeopardizing her chances for the transfer.

It was good that Eric was now in New York visiting his parents. And it was good he wouldn't be back until Sunday. That would give her three days to clear him from her mind. Three days to get back on track, forget taking lessons in self-defense and making love late into the night. From now on, her energy and concentration would be focused on her job.

It had to be that way.

Tuesday night, as students began to arrive at the dojo, Eric kept watch for Ashley. He knew something was wrong. For two days now she'd avoided him— gone to bed early; left her apartment early. Not that he'd expected her to stay up for him Sunday night, but he had thought she'd be awake when he stopped by Monday night. His knocks, however, had brought no response.

The outside door opened, and he held his breath, waiting to see who would come in. His heart rate increased when Virginia, Ashley's secretary, stepped into the building. Shyly, she smiled at him. Right behind her came another woman from Stedfeld's. Eric couldn't remember her name, just that she worked in the art department. Ashley had brought both of them with her the week before. Before they'd left, both had signed up for lessons.

The two walked on toward the dressing room, and he waited, hoping Ashley was just slower coming in, taking her time parking the car.

Anything.

At seven o'clock, with his students lined up on the mat, Eric knew Ashley wasn't coming. He went through the motions of teaching, but his mind and heart were not fully engaged. Too many questions needed to be answered, the most important being, what had happened while they were apart?

He had sensed a tension in Ashley even before Thanksgiving, but she had said it was nothing, that she was just tired. From what she'd told him about her mother, he'd suspected it had more to do with having to spend four days with her family.

At the last minute he'd invited her to fly to New York with him and spend the holiday with his parents. His father, he knew, would be busy—he always was when they came to the States on short notice—but his mother would have loved having Ashley around.

Ashley, however, had said no, that she owed it to her parents to spend the holiday with them.

All the time he was in New York, he'd thought about her, wondered what she was doing and how she was. His parents had noticed his preoccupation, and finally he had told them about Ashley. He hadn't said he loved her, but he had said he liked her. And he'd told them about her plans to move to Chicago.

His father had said that if he wanted something, he should go after it. His mother had waited until the next day, when they were alone, to talk to him.

Actually, she'd told him a story of her childhood, about the day a beautiful little bird, a *kotori*, landed on her balcony. Day after day it returned, and soon she began to look forward to seeing her *kotori*, certain it was a gift from the heavens. Her father suggested she catch it and cage it, but she could not bring herself to cage such a beautiful, free spirit. One day it flew away, and she never saw it again. She told Eric of the great emptiness she'd felt in her heart, but that she had also felt happiness.

His mother did not ask if he understood what she was saying, but he did. To love something was to let it be what it was meant to be. He had to be prepared for the day his *kotori* flew away.

Ashley hadn't flown away, though. Not yet. On Wednesday Eric left his apartment earlier than usual and drove to the address he'd looked up for Stedfeld's, Inc. For a public-relations firm he found the offices rather subdued. A receptionist directed him down a long hallway to Ashley's office.

Virginia sat at a desk outside the office. She hadn't heard him, so he cleared his throat. She looked up, her eyes growing wide. "Sensei, what are you doing here?"

"Virginia-san." He bowed. "I have come to see Ashley-san. Is she in?"

"Yes." Virginia glanced at her telephone. "But she's on a conference call. I'm not sure how much longer it will last."

"I will wait," he said, and stepped back to look at the photos hanging on the wall by Ashley's closed door.

There were pictures of Ashley shaking hands with men in tailored suits, a smiling Ashley accepting an award, and Ashley cutting the ribbon across a bridge. Eric glanced at each, and Virginia went back to the work on her desk. She didn't notice when he edged close to Ashley's door. Didn't hear when he turned the knob. And she didn't know when he slipped into Ashley's office.

Even Ashley was unaware of his presence until she hung up the phone. The moment she saw him, she gasped, her hand going to her mouth. "How long have you been standing there?"

"Not long." He nodded. "How are you?"

"Okay . . . I guess." Her gaze slid down over his black clothing; then she smiled tentatively. "You gave me a start."

Following Japanese custom, he bowed in deference. "Please forgive me. I did not mean to frighten you. I only wanted to see where you worked."

He walked toward her desk, amazed she could find anything in the jumble of papers that covered it. As he neared, she stood, pushing back her chair. She did it casually, smoothly, straightening the skirt of her blue suit as she did, and he was impressed. It was a good move. She was making certain she wasn't trapped, that she had an escape.

Only he didn't want her escaping . . . or feeling the need to escape. He stopped a few steps away. "We missed you in class last night."

"I was busy," she said, avoiding eye contact. "The VanGuard job is taking more time than I'd expected."

"But it is going well?" he asked, carefully taking another step closer. "They like what you are doing?"

"Oh, yes." Ashley could say that in all honesty. Just that afternoon the CEO of VanGuard had called personally and complimented her on the work she'd done. She had lied, though, when she'd said she'd been working the night before. The truth was, she'd accomplished nothing, other than to realize how futile it was to block Eric from her thoughts.

"Your secretary and the other woman you brought in before Thanksgiving were in class last night. I want you to know, I appreciate you getting them interested."

"You're the one who said all women should know some self-defense." As soon as she said it, Ashley knew she'd left herself open. Quickly, she went on. "Virginia said there were quite a few people there last night."

"There were," he said, and took another step toward her. "Still, I missed you."

He was getting much too close. Trying to appear casual, she turned and walked over to her bookshelf. "I've mentioned the class to others," she said, pretending to look for a book. "Who knows how many you'll get from Stedfeld's."

"Will you be in class on Thursday?"

"I, ah . . ." She pushed the book she'd pulled out

back into place, trying to think of a good excuse why she'd have to miss Thursday's class—a reason why she couldn't come to any more classes, couldn't see him, couldn't make love with him, ever again.

Vainly, she groped for a plausible excuse. For some reason, when she came back from seeing her parents, she'd thought it would be easy to cut Eric out of her life. She'd been able to do it with the other men she'd known. The moment she'd sensed her work was suffering because of her extracurricular activities, she'd called it quits and severed all ties.

The longer Eric had been away, though, the more she'd missed him. And the closer Sunday had come, the more she'd wavered in her decision.

Sunday night, when she heard him return to his apartment, she'd wanted to go to him. She had hardly slept at all that night, yet she'd still been awake the next night when he knocked on her door. His soft raps had brought tears to her eyes, and only by focusing her thoughts on her father—remembering his enthusiasm when she'd said she might be working in Chicago— was she able to stay in her bed.

"Ashley?"

The sound of Eric's soft voice, so warm and close, jarred her back to the moment. Turning, she found him only inches away, his dark eyes boring into hers— seeing far more than she wanted him to see.

"What has happened between us?" he asked.

"Nothing," she lied, looking down, afraid he could see the longing and guilt tearing at her.

Hooking a finger under her chin, he tilted her face up so she had to look at him. "Nothing is when two people who have been lovers greet each other with a kiss. When they cannot wait to see each other, to tell each other all that has happened while they were apart. Nothing is not what has happened."

She wanted to look away, but his hand—gentle yet firm—forced her to keep her gaze locked with his. "I've—I've just been very busy."

He didn't speak, but she could feel his thoughts reaching out to her, demanding the truth, not lies. In the dark depths of his eyes she saw concern, and through his finger flowed the warmth of compassion.

"You make me forget," she said, the raspy near-whisper of her voice surprising her.

"Forget?"

"What I have to do."

"And what must you do, Ashley-san?"

Staring at his face—at the mouth she knew could tease and pleasure—she licked her lips without thinking. "I have to . . ."

Her words drifted off, and she reached out to touch him, her fingertips hesitantly brushing over the rough texture of his jacket. He was darkness and light, a shadow that wouldn't go away. A dream too real to ignore. The devil, come to test and torment her.

And she was a mere mortal, too weak and powerless to fight the hold he had on her. She'd thought she could push him to the back of her mind, but he refused to stay there. "I have to get that transfer," she whispered. "I have to go to Chicago."

"If you must, then you will," he said softly, drawing her closer. "I will not hold you from your destiny, *kotori*."

She couldn't keep her hands off him, and the irony of her behavior made her laugh. "The problem is, I also want to be with you."

"And I want to be with you, for however long or short a time that might be."

"Oh, Eric, I don't know what to do." Rising up on her toes, she slipped her arms around his neck and sighed her surrender. "I've missed you."

"And I have missed you."

He wrapped his arms around her, drawing her close, and lowered his head toward hers. Just before their lips touched, someone knocked on her door. Before either could move or say a word, the door opened, and Virginia stepped into the office. "Guess who was here?" she said, looking first toward Ashley's desk. "The sensei. He—"

She stopped when she saw them in the corner. Instantaneously, Virginia's cheeks flamed red. 'I, ah . . . I'm, ah . . . Sorry."

She backed out of the room and pulled the door shut. Ashley laughed, suddenly giddy with happiness. "I take it she didn't know you were in here?"

"I sort of slipped in."

"Just sort of, huh? I can imagine."

His eyes sparkling with amusement, he brought her back close to his body. "I have been imagining things for nearly a week. It is time for a little reality."

She didn't ask what that reality was. His kisses told her all that needed to be said. Kisses of tenderness and passion, of pleasure and longing. Only when his breathing became ragged did he pull back. Both of them knew they could go no further, that her office was not the place to make love. Later that night, in her bed, they finally finished what they had begun, the need and longing satisfied. Not until the next morning, while Eric lazily watched from her bed as she dressed for work, did the feelings of guilt once again hit Ashley.

Only a week earlier she'd told her father she would soon be working in Chicago. Why then was she getting herself more and more involved with a man who was putting down roots in Ann Arbor? Why couldn't she control this desire to be with Eric? Why couldn't she forget him?

Why did she, even now, want to crawl back in bed with him and spend the morning—the entire day— with him?

She had to fulfill her promise, didn't she?

"Eric," she said, turning to face him, the loop earring she held in her hand poised halfway to her ear. "I—"

He'd levered himself up on one elbow to watch her, his dark hair mussed and a sensual look in his eyes, and all thoughts of ending their affair disappeared.

"I, ah . . ." she stammered, no longer certain what she wanted to say. Quickly, she cleared her throat. "I was wondering . . ."

"Yes?"

He got out of bed in one smooth, flowing action, his graceful movements so like a dancer's. Not bothering to dress, he started toward her.

A flick of her gaze took in all of his manly attributes, and she knew she wasn't the only one who was still thinking of making love. "Eric?" she said, a little more cautiously.

"Yes," he repeated, the word almost a promise.

"I . . ." She stopped him at arm's length. "In a couple of weeks Stedfeld's is having its annual Christmas party. Would you like to go with me?"

"A Christmas party?" He grinned, his hands playing over the sleeves of her white blouse, up her arms to her shoulders.

"It's on a Saturday," she went on, her thoughts beginning to scatter. "I know you have a class from seven to eight-thirty, but the party doesn't start until nine, and most people don't show up until nine-thirty or later. If you want to go, I wouldn't mind arriving late."

"How about work?" he asked. "How do you feel about arriving late to work?"

"Late?" The idea was so foreign, she had to repeat it. "You mean like . . . ?"

"Today. This morning."

"I've never. I couldn't—"

His lips touched hers, and she knew she could.

ELEVEN

Ashley was certain her secretary saw through her excuse for arriving late that morning, but Virginia only smiled and said nothing. In fact, Eric's name didn't come up until a week later.

Rod stopped by her office while Virginia was taking a letter. "You want a ride to the party Saturday night?" he asked.

Looking up from the papers on her desk, Ashley shook her head. "Thanks, Rod, but I'm going with my neighbor."

"Aha." He grinned. "I hope you know you're going to break my daughter's heart. She's still got a crush on that guy."

"Eric and I are just friends," Ashley insisted, glancing at Virginia. "Just friends."

Virginia merely nodded, her pencil poised over

her shorthand tablet. But after Rod left, she said, "If you're looking for a dress, Hudson's has some on sale that will knock his eyes out." She smiled. "Not that he can keep his eyes off you as it is."

"We're just friends, neighbors," Ashley repeated. "And what I need for that party is something that'll impress the boss, not Eric. Something that will portray me as levelheaded with just a flair for the imaginative. Something conservative yet festive."

The night of the party Ashley decided festive described the dress she'd bought, but definitely not conservative. She was also sure it *would* knock Eric's eyes out.

Blue had always been her color, and she loved the feel of satin. Actually, considering how much the dress cost versus its simplicity, it should have been made of gold. But gold wouldn't have draped as sexily over her shoulders or flowed as sleekly over her breasts or skimmed her hips like a second skin.

She also liked how the short length made her legs look long and sleek. The three-inch heels on the satin shoes she'd had dyed to match the dress would add to that illusion, though she was sure she'd be cursing those heels before the night was over.

She left her hair down, the way Eric liked it, put on the dangling blue-and-gold enameled earrings that had caught her eye in a boutique near Michigan's campus, a blue velvet choker she'd bought the summer before at a yard sale, and three of her favorite rings.

Finally, she dabbed on a little of the perfume she'd purchased just that afternoon.

Her credit card balance, she knew, would be horrendous come January, but when she opened her front door for Eric, she didn't care. His eyes did everything a woman wanted a man's eyes to do. Grinning, she turned so he could get the full effect. "You like?"

"I like," he said huskily, then cleared his throat. "Sorry I am late."

"No problem."

Especially considering how *he* looked. She didn't know what he'd paid for his suit, but as far as she was concerned, it was also worth every penny it had cost.

It was different from American suits, the lack of lapels on the jacket giving it an Oriental look. The fabric appeared incredibly soft, the color a deep, rich black. He wore his customary black turtleneck beneath it, and the effect was suave and mysterious.

Her stomach curled, and she knew she'd better hurry and get her coat or they wouldn't be leaving her apartment.

It was nearly ten when they arrived at the hotel where the party was being held. Their overcoats left on a rack, Eric and she paused just inside the banquet room and took a moment to look around.

A portable wet bar had been set up in one corner, and a long buffet table was nearby, its surface covered with platters of food and an ice sculpture of Santa Claus. In the far corners were a gaily decorated Christmas tree and a four-piece combo that was playing a medley of holiday pieces. Above their heads long red and green tinsel garlands were strung from the center of the ceiling to the room's corners, and in front of them were several small tables, each decorated with a mixture of evergreen boughs and colorful ornaments.

In the subdued lighting Ashley noticed that only one couple was dancing, while everyone else was either seated at a table or standing around, downing drinks and food, talking and laughing. She'd hoped they could slip into the party without being noticed, but it wasn't to be.

Virginia saw them first and waved, her gaze immediately locking on Eric. Then Jill from the art department spied them. She said something to the woman next to her, who in turn said something to the woman next to her.

As Ashley guided Eric to the bar, more and more heads turned their way, hushed words being exchanged. "I think we're being talked about," she whispered.

"And does that bother you?" Eric asked. He was accustomed to stares and talk and an occasional incident of prejudice. He knew his being with Ashley might raise a few eyebrows. His worry was if she was having second thoughts about inviting him.

"Bother me?" She slipped her arm possessively through his. "No. But as yummy as you look tonight, I bet more women from this company start coming to your dojo."

"Yummy." He relaxed and chuckled at her choice of words. "If I had known it was that easy to get students, I would have been attending parties on a regular basis."

"It's about time you two made it," a male voice called from behind them.

A smile immediately crossed her face, and Eric knew it was someone she liked and was comfortable with. When they turned to face the man, Eric also recognized him.

"Better late than never, you know," Ashley answered. "Eric, you remember Rod, don't you? You met him at my party."

"Of course." Eric bowed slightly and shook Rod's hand. "The one whose daughter took my class."

"She was green with envy when I said I'd met you. You seem to have quite an effect on women." Rod added to Ashley, "Virginia and Jill have been telling everyone that he's 'awesome,' to quote them. And Virginia swears he can walk through walls."

Ashley grinned at Eric. "Who knows, maybe he can. Rod, you and your daughter should come by Eric's dojo sometime, watch him in action. In fact, take some classes."

Eric laughed. "I think she is trying to drum up business for me tonight. But you are welcome any time."

"We might just drop by." Again Rod turned to Ashley, lowering his voice to a near whisper. "Old Jimbo's playing it risky tonight."

Quickly, she glanced around the room. "How's that?"

"He's hitting the sauce pretty hard. I think what happened with June along with your latest coup really has him sweating."

Ashley shook her head. "I don't know. He swears

he never touched June, and as aggressive as that woman was, he might be telling the truth. But I don't understand how he could have messed up so badly on that ad copy. If it had gone to press as it was, someone's head would have rolled."

"Well, your quick thinking made points with the boss, and Jim knows it."

"Now, all I have to do is keep from making any mistakes myself."

Eric noticed her glance his way and knew she considered their relationship a mistake. She was fighting her feelings, and her confusion tore at him. He knew how she felt in his arms, how she gave with total passion, yet there were times when he could feel her pulling away, could read the guilt and indecision in her eyes. She was drawn to him, but her obsession to get the transfer to Chicago had not lessened.

"From what I've heard," she said, "the selection is down to four. A guy from Indiana, a woman from Wisconsin, and Jim and me. The decision will be made sometime after the new year, so you guys cross your fingers for me."

She crossed her own fingers, but Eric was sure she didn't need any extra help. If she was as quick and attentive on her job as she was with her lessons in his classes, she would be the one selected. Then she would be gone . . . and all he would have would be memories.

As she talked to Rod, Eric thought back to his mother's story. Ashley was indeed like a little bird— her voice soft and musical, her song so sweet. A bluebird tonight. So beautiful and sexy. His *kotori* that he had the pleasure of knowing and loving, if only for a short while.

He kept telling himself he would be able to let her go when the time came. Yet, somehow, with her by his side, with the soft scent of her perfume and the alluring essence of her teasing him to distraction, he wondered how.

"Rod, I don't want to talk business tonight," Ashley said, and Eric brought his attention back to the conversation. She grinned up at him. "My awesome neighbor and I are going to enjoy a party."

Rod chuckled and again shook hands with him. "Hope you know what a gem this gal is. She's going far."

Eric didn't need the man reminding him.

They got drinks from the bar and food from the table, and he had to admit, as they mingled with the others at the party, Ashley tried not to talk business. When one man asked her a question about a layout she'd given him the day before, she told him she'd go over it with him on Monday. When a woman apologized for not finding time to get the data on new growth in the Ann Arbor area, Ashley told her they were at a party and not to worry. But when an older man with a short haircut who was wearing a conservative gray suit walked toward them, Eric knew from the way Ashley tensed that this was someone important.

"Wonderful party, Wayne," she said. "May I introduce my escort, Eric Newman. Eric, this is Wayne Martin, vice president of Stedfeld's and the boss man of our branch."

Wayne Martin, Eric decided after a few minutes of conversation, was a man who enjoyed his position and believed in the hierarchy of power. When he asked what Ashley thought about thirty-second spots on prime time for a client, Eric wasn't surprised when she didn't put him off until Monday but answered the question.

After her boss left, she apologized. "I'm sorry. You've got to be totally bored."

"Not at all." Actually, he'd found the conversation interesting. "Your ideas are good."

She glanced over her shoulder, in the direction her boss had taken. "Let's just hope Wayne thinks so."

"And if he does not?"

"When the screening committee is ready to make the final decision on that position, they'll contact him. He'll be the one who recommends either Jim or me. And though Jim's made a few mistakes lately, he's been around for a lot of years and is good friends with Wayne. Me, I'm still virtually a newcomer. Every idea I present counts, everything I do or say. One mistake and Wayne will recommend Jim over me. I know he will."

"And you would be stuck here." Eric studied her delicate face—her blue eyes so full of sparkle, her mouth so tempting. Leaning close, he brushed a kiss against the soft halo of her hair. "Would staying in Ann Arbor be so terrible?" he asked softly.

"Terrible?"

Ashley wished she could say yes. The problem was, in the last five years, she'd actually grown to love Ann Arbor. It was a city of many faces. High tech mixed with an academic atmosphere. Casual sophistication. A breath of fresh air in contrast to big-city life.

And Eric was in Ann Arbor.

No, staying wouldn't be terrible . . . if it were up to her. "What would be terrible," she said, "would be if I let my father down."

"Your father?"

Eric frowned, and she wasn't sure how to explain. Looking away, she tried to think, but then she saw Jim Stanton headed toward them. "Uh-oh," she muttered under her breath. The way Jim was glaring at her, she knew he wasn't bringing holiday wishes.

"Well, well, well," Jim said with a sneer. "If it isn't the little tattletale." He scowled at her, then turned his gaze to Eric.

Ashley could almost see the wheels spinning in the man's head as he measured Eric's slight build against his own height and muscular body. Jim liked to brag about how much he worked out and how he was in as good shape now as he'd been in college. The way he was looking at Eric, she knew he was underestimating what he was seeing.

"And is this your foreign guard dog?" he asked.

"This is my neighbor and friend, Eric Newman," she answered, hoping to avoid a scene. "Eric, this is Jim Stanton."

Eric held out his hand, but Jim ignored it. Instead, he aggressively rested his hands on his hips and cynically looked Eric up and down. "I've heard the talk about you, and I'm not impressed. You don't look all that 'awesome.'"

"I never said I was," Eric said calmly, but Ashley

noticed he set his drink on a table so his hands were free.

"Well, that's all I've been hearing about you." Jim glanced toward her. "Your secretary's been saying he's a ninja warrior, talks about him like he was a god."

"Believe me," Eric said, bringing Jim's attention back to him, "I am very mortal."

"Oh, I bet you are." Jim sneered again. "Put us on a mat, and I'd have you pinned in thirty seconds."

Perhaps to emphasize his point, Jim poked a finger at Eric's chest. Except Eric easily angled his body back and to the side, and Jim's finger and hand slipped by, touching nothing but air.

Immediately, Jim's eyes narrowed into a penetrating glare, and his stance became even more hostile.

He jutted his chin out, and Ashley knew she had to put a stop to this. She laid a hand on Jim's arm. "People are looking at us," she said, keeping her voice hushed.

Jim glanced at the people who were watching them, then smiled smugly and called out, "Tell me, does this guy really look so awesome?"

He didn't wait for an answer but shrugged off her hand and edged closer to Eric. "*Me*, I was a wrestler in high school and college. I always wondered how I'd do against one of you Oriental fighters."

"You wouldn't have a chance," Ashley said, afraid he was going to try. "Don't fight him, Eric. He's drunk."

"I am not going to fight him," he assured her, and took another step back. But she knew by his stance that he was ready.

"Too chicken?" Jim asked cockily. He walked forward, and again Eric stepped back.

The combo continued to play "White Christmas," but around them conversations had stopped, and Ashley could feel all eyes focused on them.

The people behind Eric moved aside when he took yet another step back. He was angling his body away from the tables and toward the door.

"You are a chicken," Jim said. "In wrestling, when a guy keeps backing up, he's penalized points. You can't win if you lose points."

"There are different levels of winning," Eric said.

Ashley knew Jim couldn't stand to lose on any level, and that it wasn't going to be long before he made his move. She had to do something, and quickly. So she stepped between the two of them. "Jim, think about where we are. You don't want to start a fight."

To stop him, she put her hands on his chest, but he pushed them away and shoved her back against Eric. "What should I do then?" he asked bitterly, glaring at her. "Kiss up, the way you do? Sleep my way to the top?"

Before she could respond, Eric's hands were at her waist and he was moving her to the side. "I think it is time for you to leave now," he said to Jim, his tone lethally level.

"You gonna make me?"

Once again Jim reached forward, this time to push Eric, and Ashley groaned. Before Jim's hand reached Eric's chest, Eric was beside him, catching Jim's arm and twisting it behind his back. She knew from the little she'd learned in her self-defense class just how disabling a wrist hold could be. She wasn't surprised when Jim's attitude immediately changed, fear filling his eyes and a whimper escaping his lips.

"Don't break my arm," he begged.

"Then do not fight me," Eric said firmly. "Did you come with someone?"

"My wife."

Ashley could see Teri Stanton standing by the buffet table, biting her lower lip and wringing her hands. She also saw Wayne Martin striding across the room toward them, his expression grim.

"I think it is time for you and your wife to call it a night," Eric said, but he turned Jim toward her, and Ashley found herself looking into watery gray eyes.

"Apologize to her," Eric demanded. "For all you said."

Jim didn't hesitate. "I apologize," he mewled, and she suddenly felt sorry for him. In spite of his size and bravado, he wasn't half the man Eric was.

"Problem?" Wayne asked as he reached them, his gaze darting from Ashley to Jim to Eric.

Without loosening his hold on Jim, Eric shook his head. "Just helping a man get his coat."

Wayne looked back at Jim. "Do you need any help getting your coat?"

"No," Jim said, the word almost a plea.

"I think he'll be fine now," Wayne said. Jim's wife had come up beside him. He patted her arm. "You can help him get his coat, can't you, Teri?"

Teri immediately agreed. Ashley held her breath, not sure what Eric would do. The panther had his prey.

To her relief he released his hold on Jim's wrist and stepped back beside her.

Jim rubbed his arm, glaring at them. "You caught me off guard," he said, then repeated it louder, for all to hear. "He caught me off guard. That's all."

Ashley knew better.

She wasn't sure what Wayne thought, but he judiciously stepped between Jim and Eric. "It's a shame you have to leave so early," he said to Jim. "I'll walk you and Teri to the door."

It wasn't until the three of them had walked away that Ashley dared relax. Closing her eyes, she sighed.

"Are you all right?" Eric asked, touching her arm.

Was she?

Forcing a smile, she looked at him. "You were fantastic. But . . ." Again, she sighed. "I should have realized Jim would carry his resentment over what happened the other day to tonight. You tell us in class to know what we're getting into before we enter a situation. I should have known he would act like this and should have stayed away tonight."

"But you had every right to be here."

"Maybe so. The question is, what is Wayne going to think?"

Eric studied her for a moment, then glanced toward the doorway. She also looked in that direction and could see Jim and his wife near the coatrack, talking to Wayne. Laughing.

"It does not matter who was right or wrong, just what your boss thinks?" Eric asked.

"It matters who Wayne recommends. And whose story he believes."

"If he is a wise man, you will be the one your boss chooses."

She wasn't sure how wise Wayne Martin was.

After that, the party lost its festive edge, and Ashley knew she had to get away. She was glad when Eric agreed that it was time to leave. Even Wayne seemed relieved when she said they were going. He said his good-byes pleasantly, but she noticed he didn't walk with her to the door, not as he had with Jim.

On the drive back to the apartment building, neither of them said much. After Eric parked his car, though, he put a hand on her arm, stopping her from getting out. "I know you are concerned about what happened tonight, and I am sorry."

"It wasn't you," she said. "You did what you had to do. Actually, you handled the situation beautifully. I just . . ."

She stopped, unsure what she wanted to say, and he gently squeezed her arm. "Why is it so important for you to go to Chicago, Ashley?"

"Because . . ." In the darkness she shrugged, not knowing how to explain . . . or if she could. "Because I made a promise that I would."

"Who did you promise?"

"Someone I can't let down."

"Your father?"

"My father and . . ." Suddenly uncomfortable with the direction the conversation was going, she pulled back. "Look, I really don't want to talk about this. Let's go inside."

He held on to her arm. "In a minute. Why do you not ever want to talk about this?"

"I just don't." She could feel the tension building within her. It always did when she remembered. And the air in his car was becoming exceedingly close, making breathing difficult.

"Ashley, I ask you again. Why is it so important for you to go to Chicago?"

"Because it's a dream that needs to be fulfilled. Eric, I'm going inside," she insisted, and turning her wrist, she pulled free from his hold and opened her door.

He was beside her before she reached the front of his car. "What are you running from?" he asked.

"I'm not running from anything." But she was close to a run as she crossed the street.

He stayed with her. "Is this a dream or a nightmare?"

She cringed at how close he was to the truth. "A dream. You just wouldn't understand."

She went through the door first, but they climbed the stairs together, his steps barely sounding. He walked with her to her door and stopped her from slipping inside. "I understand many things, Ashley. I see a woman who cannot slow down, who drives herself to reach a goal she cannot talk about. There is something wrong."

"There's nothing wrong," she said, yet knew it was a lie. So much was wrong, she couldn't even face it.

He said nothing for a moment; then finally he nodded. "Well, if you ever do want to talk about it . . ."

"I'll give you a call," she promised, and managed a smile.

TWELVE

Eric knew he could not push Ashley for the reason why going to Chicago was so important. To push would achieve nothing. He'd seen the pain in her eyes and knew it was more than ambition. More than a dream.

He decided to spend as much time with her as he could. He was certain once she trusted him, she would confide in him. But the next morning, as he read through the Sunday edition of the Ann Arbor *News*, his plans changed.

The article about the two burglaries was on the third page near the bottom. It was the locations of the robberies that first caught his attention. One had happened only a block from his dojo, the other not far from his apartment building. One victim's statement that she'd had her purse stolen only the month before prompted him to pick up the phone.

When Eric didn't stop by Sunday or Monday night, Ashley was afraid he was angry with her. Then on Tuesday night, when she went to class and the black belt who greeted them said Eric had been called out of town, she worried about why Eric was gone—and why he hadn't told her he was leaving. Then Wednesday night, when she stayed up until after midnight working on a speech she had to give at a luncheon, she was certain she heard someone in Eric's apartment. Nevertheless, Thursday night the black belt announced that Eric was still out of town.

On Friday Charlie said he'd seen Eric.

"It was early this morning," he told her. "Very early. Maybe four o'clock."

She didn't ask him what he'd been doing up at that hour. She'd seen Edie Wyconski drop by Charlie's apartment more than once.

"He was just coming in," Charlie said. "All dressed in black, as usual, with even a black stocking face mask. You know the kind, with just the holes for your eyes and mouth."

Charlie's eyebrows rose slightly, saying more than words might. "He looked surprised to see me. Kinda upset. Whaddaya think's up?"

She didn't know what to think.

Not until three days later, when Lieutenant Pease called her office and asked her to drop by the station. He'd like to see if she could identify a couple of teenage boys.

A clerk at the front desk helped Ashley when she arrived at the police station. "Lieutenant Pease said you'd be in." She motioned for Ashley to follow her. "These boys hit your place?"

"My place?" she asked, confused.

"Burglary."

"No, but they may be the ones who stole my purse a couple of months ago."

"Then you're lucky, honey. They would have probably gotten you one of these days if they hadn't gone off the deep end." She glanced back at Ashley. "They're a pair of druggies, if you ask me. Comin' in here swearin' a phantom haunts the streets, sayin' he took things right out from under their noses." The woman shook her head.

"They ever see this phantom?" Ashley asked. She suspected she knew what—or who—had been haunting the streets of Ann Arbor.

"They said no, but still they swore there was one." She led Ashley to a small room and motioned for her to go in. "The lieutenant will be with you in a minute." She chuckled. "I don't know what them boys saw or didn't see, but whatever it was sure scared the bejeebies out of them. When they came in here, they confessed everything."

Ashley grinned. Being stalked by a panther, she was sure, could loosen a person's tongue.

She wasn't the least bit surprised that the two boys were the same ones who had roughed her up and taken her purse. Willingly, she identified them.

"Seems they kept the keys from the purses they stole," the lieutenant told her. "Tagged each with the owner's address . . . for a later visit. I'm sure yours are among the ones we picked up. We'll get them back to you as soon as possible."

She thanked him and left. The next night, when Eric dropped by, apologizing for having had to leave town on such short notice and bringing her a Christmas gift, she also thanked him. Not that he admitted he was the phantom the boys claimed stalked the streets, but she knew he was. Especially when, soon after the first of the year, both boys started working at the dojo . . . and taking classes. She asked Eric if that was wise. His answer was simple. "To go in a new direction, you must start on a new path."

Watching the way he worked with the boys, she soon believed that if anyone could give them a new start, it would be Eric. Oh, they would fight him for a while. Resist, as she had. They might even think they could ignore him. But in the end he would win.

Hadn't he stolen her heart?

She wasn't sure exactly when she fell in love with him. At Christmas she was still denying it, still telling herself she was simply enjoying his company, that when the time came to leave, she'd have no problems. Her New Year's resolution was that, no matter if she got the transfer or not, she'd be working in Chicago by summer. It really wasn't until the day Wayne Martin called her into his office to announce who had gotten the transfer to Chicago that the truth hit.

That night, during class, she couldn't keep her eyes off Eric. A part of her wanted to shout to everyone on the mat, "I love this man."

Another part of her was fighting tears.

After class she went home, while Eric taught his advanced class. Alone in her apartment, she fixed dinner for the two of them and did cry. Then she put on fresh makeup and dressed especially for Eric.

She hoped he would like what she'd cooked. Not one item had been bought at a fast-food restaurant or from the grocery's frozen section. She put a tablecloth on the table, too, and created a centerpiece of candles and flowers. By ten-thirty, when Eric knocked on her door, everything was ready. She had the lights turned down low, a romantic tape playing, a bottle of champagne on ice, and the candles lit.

"Ashley-san," he said, looking around as he removed his shoes, and she closed the door behind him. "If I did not know better, I might think you were trying to seduce me."

"Beware," she said teasingly, knowing if she didn't keep things light, she was going to be hit by another deluge of tears. "You are about to be attacked by a sex-starved woman."

She wrapped her arms around his neck and rose on to her toes, pressing her body against his so her baggy blue sweater and formfitting black stretch pants became one with his black sweater and jeans.

"Do I fear for my life?" he asked huskily, his hands clasping her waist.

She could feel the stirrings of desire in him and provocatively rubbed her hips against his, bringing about an even greater response. "Your life will be spared, but your virtue is definitely in danger," she whispered near his lips.

She expected him to kiss her and was totally unprepared when he swept the sole of his foot against her ankles, taking her feet out from under her. The moment she began to fall, he tightened his hold on her waist and brought her gently down onto the carpet. Using one hand to pin her arms above her head and his legs to hold hers secure, he stretched out over her.

"Unfair," she squealed, wiggling beneath him.

"Perfectly fair," he assured her. "Now, it is you who is under my power."

Gazing into his eyes, she knew the truth. "I've been under your power since the first day we met."

"I wish." He chuckled and kissed her lips. "I could hardly wait for class to end so I could be here."

"Poor boy." She feigned concern. "Are you that hungry?"

"Hungry for you." Again he kissed her, this time his mouth not as gentle, and the pressure of his hips against hers confirming the truth of his words.

As his lips played over hers, his free hand slid down to the bottom of her sweater, then under the soft knit to touch her skin. His fingers, so strong yet so tender, slowly traveled up over her ribs, and shivers of anticipation raced through her, her body tensing with desire.

"Ah," he murmured, discovering no bra to keep

him from her breasts. For a moment he arched back to gaze into her eyes; then he smiled. "I like."

And so did she. Oh, how she liked the gentle kneading of his fingers, the warmth of his hand, and the passion of his kisses. Each touch, each caress, soothed and excited at the same time.

This was the man she loved.

She hadn't wanted to love him; she'd thought she had everything under control. Somehow love had sneaked up on her, penetrated her defenses. Now, the idea filled her, turning her insides to liquid fire.

"I love you," she whispered, awed by the sound of the words.

He released his hold on her arms and sat back on her legs, staring down at her. "You mean it?"

"Yes." With all her heart and soul.

"And I love you," he said fervently, the look in his eyes echoing the emotion.

"Then make love to me," she begged. "Wild, passionate love."

"Gladly." He pulled her sweater over her head and tossed it aside. Hungrily, his gaze caressed her nakedness, than he smiled in satisfaction. "I love every part of you."

Inching down, he straddled her, leaning forward to draw one taut nipple into his mouth. She groaned and ran her fingers through his thick hair, delighting in each kiss he gave her, each lick of his tongue.

I love you. Love you. Love you.

Over and over the words sang through her head. It was wild and exciting. Frightening.

He caressed and suckled her breasts; then his

hands dropped lower, to the waistband of her stretch pants, and his kisses traveled a path to her navel. She held her breath when he lowered her pants, the tension within her turning to sweet agony. Slowly, inch by inch, he exposed the triangle of taffy-colored hair that curled between her legs, and just as slowly he feathered little kisses over her stomach, each dropping lower.

Anticipation caught her breath, her heart racing when he paused to draw her pants and panties down to her ankles, then off. Starting with her toes, he worked his way back up, each teasing kiss bringing him closer to the apex of her desire; each lick of his tongue moistening her skin; and each tiny nibble of his teeth along the soft insides of her thighs driving her crazy, until she wanted to scream out her frustration.

She knew he was enjoying his position of power, yet she was not content to remain the passive one. Just before he made her his total prisoner, she acted. She banked on Eric being caught off guard and moved quickly, using her feet and legs along with the weight of her body. In one fluid turn she reversed their positions, straddling his chest and catching his hands as he reached out to stop her.

"Gotcha," she said smugly, pinning his arms above his head.

Eric chuckled and relaxed, not fighting her. Although she had surprised him, it would take little to regain the advantage. Only he had no desire to do so, just as he had no objections to finding a breast only inches from his mouth. "You are becoming quite the ninja, my little bird."

"And you have too many clothes on." She inched back, so her hips were closer to his. And as she did, her body flattened out, taking away what little weight advantage she'd had. She laughed. "How's a woman who's smaller than a man supposed to rape him?"

"She holds him pinned to the floor with exotic kisses." He raised his head so his lips came into quick contact with hers, then, with a contented sigh, relaxed again. "Ah, yes, I am your prisoner."

She also sighed, letting go of his arms and sitting back. "How many years would it take, Eric, before I ever had the advantage over you?"

Gently rubbing his hands on her arms, he grew very serious. "Sometimes I think you always have the advantage."

Then he grinned again and wiggled beneath her, pulling his sweater up and over his head. "I am yours," he said, stretching his arms straight out from his sides, as though they were pinned to the carpet by invisible shackles.

"Just remember that," she said, and scooted lower on his legs so she could unbutton his jeans.

"And what terrible tortures do you have planned for me?"

Not looking at him but watching his zipper, she slowly pulled it down. "Hard telling. My sensei says to let everything happen naturally."

" 'Hard' pretty much describes it," Eric agreed. "Which is natural every time I am around you."

"Poor boy."

"I am in absolute misery," he said, wishing she'd touch him, either on purpose or by accident.

"My sensei also says one should turn misery into pleasure."

"Sounds good to me." Though he certainly didn't remember ever saying that.

His misery became pure pleasure when she caressed him, first by the brush of her palm as she pulled down his jeans and briefs, then with the teasing strokes of her fingers.

He closed his eyes and soared to the realm of ecstasy as she wrapped her hand around him and leaned close to kiss him. Only when she flattened herself over him and began rubbing her hips against his, did he take any action of his own.

His arms around her, he held her close. "Slowly, my love," he whispered near her ear. "Slowly."

She did move slowly. Slowly, she positioned herself over him, and slowly, she took him in, surrounding him with her soft, liquid warmth. And then, ever so slowly, she moved with the grace of a woman, and he knew true enlightenment was to discover all you could be when giving and receiving, to be so closely in tune with another human being that every movement became as one.

When the question of which one of them had the power no longer mattered, he rolled over so she was under him. He gave himself to her, totally immersing himself in the pleasure of all she was and all she brought to his life.

Ashley clung to him, never wanting the moment

to end, relishing the feelings of complete satisfaction and contentment. Soon enough, she knew, she would have to face reality.

I love you, Eric Newman, she thought again as she shifted to lie beside him, nestled close.

It was a blessing and a curse.

How much easier it would be if she didn't love him, if she'd never let him get close to her. To have met Eric at this point in time didn't seem fair. How could she fulfill all the needs of her life?

It was too much to face, and she put off the question. "Hungry now?" she asked, idly running a fingertip over his chest.

He caught her hand and kissed her fingers. "Sated."

"And here I spent all night cooking a well-balanced, made-from-scratch, all-American meal."

He chuckled and propped himself up on one elbow. "How you have changed from the woman I met four-and-a-half months ago."

That was the problem. She had changed. "I'm definitely in better physical shape."

His gaze traveled the length of her, then his hand, his fingers grazing the firm muscles of her arms and shoulders, the soft curves of her breasts, and the flat line of her stomach. "Great shape."

"Nobody better mess with me or my purse now."

Once again he chuckled. "Just the other day, one of the boys said it was a good thing you didn't know then what you do now, or they would have been in trouble. If you get that transfer to Chicago, you should be well able to defend yourself."

Suddenly, she knew she couldn't put it off, that the time had come to tell him. Taking a deep breath, she struggled to organize her thoughts.

"About Chicago . . ." she started, then paused. He said nothing, but she felt him tense. "Wayne called me into his office today. The decision on who's to be transferred has been made."

For a moment more Eric was silent; then he tilted her chin so she was looking directly into his eyes. "You got it?"

She nodded. "Funny . . ." Again she paused, realizing how strange it really was. "In a way you helped me get the job. Rather than being upset by what happened at the Christmas party, Wayne was impressed with the way you handled Jim. And he likes it that I've been getting so many of the women in the agency to take lessons in self-defense. He said it showed true initiative. And he said the screening committee was equally impressed. So you see, I owe it all to you."

"You accepted?" Eric asked quietly.

"Yes. I start as soon as possible."

"I thought you said you loved me."

"I do." She wanted him to understand that. "Oh, Eric, I really do. But I have to go."

"So . . ." He ran his fingers through her hair, his gaze never leaving her face. "My little bird is about to fly away."

To fly away. She felt as though she were flying apart. "It doesn't mean we have to stop seeing each other." At least not if he went along with the idea she'd thought of that afternoon.

"And how do we continue seeing each other?" he asked, sitting up and reaching for his briefs.

As he put them on, Ashley reached for her own panties. "You could come to Chicago. It's really a great city. It has culture, entertainment, and sports. It's probably a lot more like the cities you've lived in than Ann Arbor is."

"Chicago is a long way from here," he said, and grabbed his jeans.

Since he seemed intent on getting dressed, she pulled on her stretch pants. "It's not that far, really," she said. "A four-hour drive. Sometimes less, if you put the pedal to the metal."

Standing, he pulled up his zipper. "Not far, yet very far."

"Still, after I'm gone, you could come see me. I could come back here and see you." She mentally crossed her fingers as she stood and threw out her idea. "Or you could move there."

He didn't say anything immediately, so she went on. "I know you couldn't right away, that you probably have your money all tied up in the dojo here, but maybe in a year or two? And meanwhile, we could see each other on weekends. Probably not every weekend, I'm sure I'll have to work some, but at least a couple each month."

Still he said nothing, silently studying her face. Then he shook his head. "It would not work, Ashley-san."

He was rejecting her idea. Flatly. Dashing the one hope she'd had that she could find a solution to her confusion. He'd said he loved her, but it was clear he didn't love her as much as she loved him. As he pulled on his sweater and she pulled on hers, she forced back the tears that threatened to embarrass her.

Then he touched her arm. "What if you were not to go?"

THIRTEEN

Eric knew the question was selfish, but he didn't want her to go. It didn't matter that this was a good career move for Ashley or that getting a job in Chicago had been her dream for years. It didn't even matter that she'd told him all along that she'd be going. A few hours on weekends would not be enough. He wanted her to stay.

Her answer was a shake of her head. Her long, wavy hair, tangled from their lovemaking, brushed her cheeks. "I have to go," she said.

"Have to?"

"I promised."

"Promised. Who did you promise?"

She looked down at the rug. "Jack."

Eric tried to think of a Jack Ashley had mentioned from work. Then he realized who she meant. "Your brother?"

"Yes." She looked up again, directly into his eyes. "The day he was buried, I promised him I would get a job in Chicago, get a place with a view of the lake. It was his dream. And Dad's."

"Ashley, you were ten years old when your brother died. A child. No one expects you to keep a promise like that."

"I do," she said flatly, and turned away. "After what I did, it's the only thing I can do."

She walked toward her dining table. Confused, Eric hesitated a moment, then followed. "And what did you do?"

Again she faced him. Her lips were tight together, as though holding back the words, then she took a deep breath. Her answer came as she let it out. "I killed my brother."

She said it flatly, with no emotion, but he saw tears in her eyes, and her chin began to tremble. Immediately, he touched her, grasping her hands.

"How?" he asked, keeping the shock from his voice.

"With my selfishness. My stupidity. My—"

She stopped, closing her eyes, and one tear slid down her cheek. He pulled her close, wrapping his arms around her. No matter what her guilt might be, she was suffering, and if he could take the pain away—any of it—he would, gladly.

"Oh, Eric," she cried into his sweater. "People say it wasn't my fault, but they're wrong. It was. I'm the one to blame."

"How did you kill your brother?" he repeated.

"We never should have been on the road," she

said, a distant quality to her voice. "I should have listened to my mother. Instead, all I thought was that it was one more time I wasn't going to get to do what I wanted to do. One more time I'd gotten my hopes up, only to have them dashed."

"What was it you wanted?"

"To win." She sighed. "To win a gymnastics competition. Back then, I was really good at it. At least the coach at the Y said I was. I was so sure if I could win, Dad would be proud of me, as proud as he was of Jack's successes. And that my mother would pay more attention to me. Ice on the roads meant nothing. I wanted to go."

Once again, she sighed, tilting her head up to look at him. "So I asked Jack to take me. I knew a few tears and a little pleading would get through to him."

Eric could imagine. If at ten Ashley was anywhere near as irresistible as she was now, her brother would have been putty in her hands. "So he drove you to the competition?"

She dropped her head again, and he felt her nod against his chest. "We didn't even tell Mom we were going. And, as usual, Dad was working. We just got in Jack's car and took off.

"It was getting late, so I told him to hurry. He said, 'I'll get you there, kid.' And then—"

She stopped, and the rigid feel of her body told Eric she was back in time, reliving that moment. "Ashley," he said, tightening his hold to let her know he was there for her.

She took in a deep breath, a shudder running the length of her, then drew back enough to look up at him again. When she spoke, her voice was deadly calm. "Then the car started spinning. We hit a tree. I was knocked out, suffered a mild concussion and a few bruises, but that's all. They say Jack was killed instantly."

"But, Ashley, it was not you who killed him."

"Oh, no? Then who did?" she asked, pulling out of his embrace. "If it hadn't been for me, he wouldn't have been driving that car on those icy roads, wouldn't have been going as fast as he was. Wouldn't have spun out. If it hadn't been for me, he would be alive today, living and working in Chicago, being everything he ever wanted to be."

"And you think your going to Chicago will bring him back?"

"No. But I promised him I would do this, that one day I would fulfill his dream. His dream and Dad's."

They'd gone full circle, and Eric didn't know what to say. In her mind Ashley carried the guilt of the accident. It did not matter that her brother had been eighteen at the time, old enough to know the dangers of driving on icy roads. He had died that day, leaving behind a ten-year-old girl who believed the accident was her fault. And the twenty-seven-year-old woman standing before him believed she owed it to her family to give back what she'd taken away.

What he hated most was that he understood her position. He'd been raised in the Japanese tradition. A promise was to be honored, no matter the sacrifice.

"I promised both Jack and Dad that I'd make it up to them," Ashley said, the sound of determination returning to her voice. "It's taken me longer than I thought it would, but now I've made it."

"And what does your father think of this?" Eric asked.

"I haven't told him I got the position, but I know he's going to be excited. My going to Chicago has been the only thing we've been able to talk about like father and daughter since the day Jack died. First it was an amused smile and a pat on the head when I told him I was going to get a job in one of the tall buildings downtown and live in a beautiful house where I could see the lake. Then, as I got older, it turned into questions. How did I plan on doing this? What kind of job would it be? And since I got the job with Stedfeld's, it's been, 'Any idea when?' "

"So this is for him?"

"And for Jack," she added. "I'm accomplishing what both Dad and Jack wanted, what Jack would have done if he'd lived. And maybe it's crazy, but I feel as though Jack knows."

"Why did you not tell me this before?" He had asked so many times. And so many times she'd evaded the subject.

She bowed her head. "Talking about the accident isn't easy for me, Eric. Around my house it's never mentioned. It would upset my mother too much. She was unstable before. Since Jack died, she's been worse, either blaming me for what happened or living in a fantasy world, still thinking Jack's alive. My father, well, he . . ."

She stopped, and Eric could tell she was again fighting tears. Blinking, she looked up and forced a smile. "I'm sorry. The reason I don't talk about it is, every time I do, I end up crying. So, let's change the subject. Okay?"

"Maybe you need to cry."

"Maybe," she agreed, but she wiped away the tears that had escaped and gave his arms a squeeze. "Now you know the reason why I have to go to Chicago."

"And to not go?"

"Is impossible. Only—"

Almost desperately, she rubbed her hands up and down the sleeves of his sweater, as if somehow she could erase the pain of what was to come. He knew the feelings between them were more intense than she'd ever wanted. From the very beginning she'd fought the attraction, and even when she'd given in, she'd continued to remind him that she would one day leave. Time after time, she'd insisted that they had no future. That she'd told him she loved him and suggested he move to Chicago was a big step forward. And if it were that simple, he would move.

Only life was never simple.

Suddenly, she stopped rubbing his arms and sighed. "It looks like we've come to an impasse. You don't want to go to Chicago; I have to."

"It is not a matter of not wanting to go," he said. "You are right. My money is tied up in my dojo. And my business is not the kind I can build up in a couple of years, then start in another city. To succeed, I have to make a commitment. Like you, I have made promises I cannot break."

"And so we go our separate ways." She turned and headed for her kitchen.

"I suppose," he said quickly, "we could try your idea of getting together on weekends. I could cancel my Saturday night class, drive to Chicago after the afternoon class."

She paused and looked back. "No, you were right. It wouldn't work."

Ten days later Ashley was ready to move.

Everything had happened so fast, she was still having trouble believing it. Once she told Wayne she would accept the position, nothing was the same. Her accounts were turned over to Rod and Jim; she was flown to Chicago to meet Mr. Stedfeld himself and be assigned an office; arrangements were made for her to share a condominium with another female employee— a condominium that had a view of Lake Michigan—and a moving van was scheduled to pick up her furnishings and either transfer them to her new living quarters or put them in storage.

She really had no time to see Eric, but she couldn't stay away from him. Twice she was going to skip her class at the dojo and pack, and twice she changed her mind and went, wanting that chance to see him in action again, to marvel at all he could do.

And there was the bookcase she had to dismantle. It should have come apart easily, and she could have asked Charlie for help, but somehow she ended up at Eric's door. After the shelves were stacked and tied, they made love. It was a wild coming together, physically exhausting and emotionally draining.

Afterward, lying beside him, she was nearly asleep

when his telephone rang. The moment Eric left her side, she felt an emptiness and concern. For her, late-night calls meant her mother had again tried to take her life.

Holding her breath, she listened as Eric answered the phone. His initial greeting was hesitant; then he dropped his voice. "No," he whispered. "I cannot do it. Not now."

A knot formed in her stomach, concern turning to jealousy. She hadn't even left, and he had another woman calling him. She wanted to block out his words, yet she couldn't stop herself from listening.

"Yes . . . Steve, I understand," he said quietly, "but not now."

When she realized it was not another woman, the jealousy vanished, but not the knot in her stomach. Grabbing his silk robe from a chair, she slipped it on and stole out of the bedroom to his side. He glanced her way as she neared. The darkness blurred his features, but she could still see him frown.

"Steve, I understand," he repeated, his tone switching back to normal. "Look, Ashley's here. Right here . . . Yes."

She said nothing, not even after he hung up. Eric guided her back to his futon, and together they crawled under the cover. She could feel the tension in his body, but she waited, wanting him to explain. Finally, he spoke. "That was Steve Pease. The lieutenant you met."

Saying nothing, she turned toward him, touching his arm and feeling his warmth.

"Sometimes he calls. When he needs my help."

"The help of a ninja?"

She heard his intake of breath and knew what she and Charlie had guessed was true.

"It is not something we want known."

"I understand." In movies it might be heroic; in a court of law it would be illegal. "He needs you now?"

"It can wait."

Until after she was gone. Then he would do whatever Lieutenant Pease had asked, possibly risk his life. It scared her.

Snuggling close, she pressed her cheek against his shoulder. "Be careful . . . always."

He promised he would be, but she couldn't shake the feeling that something might happen to him after she left. The night before she was to leave, she mentioned it to Charlie. "If anything should happen to Eric, you would let me know, wouldn't you?"

"Anything like . . . ?" Charlie asked.

"Like if he got hurt . . . shot." Eric's abilities constantly amazed her, but even he admitted all of his training was worthless against a gun.

"Shot?" Charlie cocked his head. "And how would he get shot?"

"Oh, a jealous lover, maybe?" she said, smiling innocently and pretending to check the contents of the box she was packing. Charlie might be pretty sure Eric worked with the police, but she wasn't going to be the one to confirm it.

"If you'd stay here," Charlie said, "in Ann Arbor, you wouldn't have to worry about that man being shot by a jealous lover."

She kept her head down and could feel Charlie's gaze on her as he sat on one of the many boxes that littered the living room. "I still don't understand why you're leaving Eric."

Straightening, she faced him again and swiped a wayward lock of hair back from her face. "I have no choice."

"No choice," Charlie repeated solemnly, and pointed to the box opposite him. "Why don't you sit down. Take a break."

She had a feeling she was in for a lecture, but she sat.

"Young lady, I don't know why you feel compelled to transfer to Chicago, but I do know you're making a mistake."

She held up a hand to stop him. "Charlie, you don't have to tell me Eric's the best thing that could have ever happened to me, and I'm a stupid fool to leave him. Don't you think I've told myself that enough times in the last two weeks?"

"So, why did you accept the damned transfer? Why are you going through with this?"

"Because I can't not go through with it. Because I have to keep my promise."

"What promise?" he asked, not understanding. "To your boss?"

"To . . ." She stopped. Although she'd told Eric about her brother, she couldn't tell Charlie. He didn't know about her mother's illness, about her father's dreams, or about that fateful day seventeen years ago. He wouldn't understand what she'd taken from her parents when Jack died.

What she could give back.

"I have to do it," she said firmly. "And, besides, it's been my dream too. I mean, I do love working in public relations . . . and this is a great career move. I love Chicago."

"And you love Eric," Charlie reminded her.

"And I love Eric." Loved him with all of her heart and soul. Loved the excitement of him and the mystery, his strength and his tenderness. "The other night, he told me a story his mother told him. About a little bird she loved, and how she wouldn't cage it but would let it go when the time came. I always wondered why Eric called me his little bird. Now, I understand. And I love him all the more for giving me the freedom to fly away."

Except, even as she said it, she couldn't get rid of the lump in her throat or stop the tears that filled her eyes. She was free to go, and she had to go, but she would not fly away without leaving a part of herself behind.

The next morning the movers came. As the men carted boxes and furniture out of her apartment, Eric walked through the door. Ashley watched him sidestep the chairs and bed in the middle of her living room and work his way toward the kitchen. In his hands he carried a large square black box that was decorated with a crane design in red and gold.

"What do you have there?" she asked, delighted to see him.

"It is nothing." He held it toward her with both hands. "A little something for your trip."

Carefully, she placed the ornate box on her counter and lifted the lid. Inside was a shallow tray filled with small appetizer-type snacks. Lifting that tray exposed another tray with more food. And beneath it was a third.

"How neat," she said and, one by one, placed the trays on top of each other, until they once again formed a box.

"In Japan," Eric explained, "when we go to work or on a trip, we carry our lunch in this manner. I thought you might like a snack as you drive."

"Pretty fancy brown-bag lunch if you ask me." Turning back to him, she wrapped her arms around his neck and gave him a kiss. "When did you find time to fix the food?"

"After you left last night. I missed you."

And she'd missed him. "My father called last night," she said, forcing herself to remember why she was leaving the man she loved. "Dad's really excited for me."

Eric frowned. "One man cannot live through another."

"Don't," she begged, closing her eyes. She didn't want platitudes. It would be too easy to accept his answer, to give in and stay.

But where would that leave her father?

"I have to go. You know I do."

"I know what you believe."

Eric looked away from her, pretending to watch the movers. How he wished she'd made a promise to him, a promise to love him, to never leave. But she hadn't. With him, she had insisted there be no promises.

Foolishly, he'd agreed to her terms.

"When do you leave?" he asked.

"Probably as soon as everything is out of here, and I've turned my key over to Charlie."

"So soon."

In silence he watched as the boxes that held her possessions were carried out of the room. He could remember the first time he'd stepped into her apartment, the party she'd held. She'd warned him then that this moment would come. He'd said he understood.

He hadn't.

Back then, he'd been attracted to her, but he hadn't realized how much she would become a part of him, hadn't suspected that being with her would give him the balance he needed and the joy that had been missing in his life. That loving her would give meaning to everything he did.

He wanted to cry out his pain, but he said nothing. From birth he'd been trained by his mother to control his emotions. And in his sixteen years of ninjitsu training, he'd learned from the grand master to remain strong, no matter what happened.

So he stayed with her, even though he wanted to run, wanted to close his eyes to the reality of what was happening and to flee the knowledge that she was truly going. Even after the movers had everything out of her apartment and had driven off, he waited while Ashley said her good-byes to Charlie and turned in her key. Then he helped her carry her suitcases down to her car.

It was snowing, small, icy-hard flakes flying through the air, the wind bitter cold. He stood with her by her car door, the moment of her departure at hand. Tenderly, he wrapped her wool scarf around her neck to block out the chill and pulled her coat snugly together in the front.

"Well," he said, gazing into eyes that had turned watery blue.

"Well," she repeated. She rubbed her glove-covered hands against the sides of his coat.

"The time has come to say our good-byes."

"I'm going to miss you," she said, not bothering to stop the tears that slid down her cheeks.

"And I will miss you."

She forced a smile, her cheeks a ruddy red from the wind and the cold. "My ninja."

"My *kotori*."

"Little bird." She tried to laugh. It came out stilted. "You'd think I'd be smart enough to fly south, not to Chicago, where the weather's no better than here."

"Call me when you get there. I want to know you are safe."

"I will," she promised, and wiped her eyes. "Eric . . . ?"

"Yes?"

"I—"

Longing filled her eyes, and he waited for her to finish.

"Be careful," she finally whispered, and he suspected that wasn't what she'd meant to say.

"Don't let anything happen to you," she went on. "Especially when you . . ." Again she hesitated, her fingers tightening on his sleeves. "You know, when you're helping Lieutenant Pease."

"I will be careful," he promised.

He felt her tremble, and he wrapped his arms around her and drew her close, wanting to warm her, to protect her forever.

"Oh, Eric."

She looked up, and he knew the pain in his heart was in hers too. He wanted to take her back inside, cage her in his apartment so she would be there for him forever and ever. But he knew he couldn't.

So he kissed her.

At first her lips were cold and stiff, but against his they rapidly warmed, growing soft and giving. He kissed her and hugged her close, and wished time would stop and he would never have to let her go.

She kissed him back, clinging to him, her mouth moving hungrily under his. She kissed him and cried, shaking with her sobs, until he, too, was crying.

He groaned when she abruptly pulled back, tearing her lips from his. She turned away, facing her car, and he saw her wipe at her cheeks. Quickly, he wiped at his, hoping if she saw any moisture, she would blame it on the wind or melted snowflakes.

"I'd better go," she said, not looking at him. "Before this snow gets any worse."

Do not go! he wanted to cry out. Reluctantly, he helped her open her door. "Drive carefully."

"I will."

"Do not forget to call me."

From inside of her car she looked up. "You'll be teaching a class about the time I'll get to Chicago."

"I canceled classes today." His mind would not have been on his teaching.

"I'll call," she promised. "Take care of yourself, Eric. And, remember, I love you."

He nodded, but he couldn't say the words back to her. Not now.

Biting her lower lip, the tears once again flowing down her cheeks, she pulled her door closed. As she started her car, he brushed new snow from her windshield. Then he stepped back and bowed.

She made a slight bow with her head, then put the car into gear. She was halfway down the street before he said what he'd really wanted to say. "*Ai shite iru.*" he whispered. "I love you."

His words were lost in the wind.

FOURTEEN

Ashley had hoped her job would keep her too busy to think about Eric, but it didn't. Two-and-a-half months after she had driven away from him, he was still on her mind. If she saw someone with Oriental features, heard music that reminded her of the *koto* harp, or saw a man dressed in black, she thought of Eric. Longed for him.

Wept for him.

She'd left him, but he had not left her.

"Promises," she grumbled as she steered her car through Chicago traffic. Never was she going to make another.

The last twenty-four hours had showed clearly what a mess the promises she'd already made could get her into. Here she was, 250 miles away from the man she loved, trying to fulfill the promises she'd made to her brother and father, and her father didn't even appreciate her sacrifice. Not one bit.

Their argument yesterday had proved that.

And why she'd promised Dean Asante she'd look at his warehouse was beyond her.

Driving through one of the worst areas in Chicago was not her idea of fun, especially when she hadn't gotten enough sleep the night before. Never would she have promised to share a condominium if she'd known about the parties her roommate liked to hold.

The only positive she could see was the weather. It was a good day to be out of the office. The sun was shining, the temperature was already up to 60 degrees, and it looked as if spring might actually be here.

Her left front tire hit a pothole, and she swore. Now that the weather had improved, it would be nice if Chicago's "road engineers" would get around to filling the potholes.

Her father was crazy to think this city was so great. It might be a marvelous place to visit, but to live in? Work in? That was a whole different ball game.

Ashley checked the warehouse fronts for the address Asante had given her and added "dangerous" to her list of negatives about Chicago. At least certain areas were, and this was one of them. The men loitering near the buildings and hanging around the parked cars didn't look like the type you'd want to take home to meet Mommy and Daddy.

Always be aware of your surroundings. she remembered Eric saying. She would be. And from now on, she wasn't promising anyone anything. Not even a client. Who cared if she saw where Asante stored his merchandise? He could have described the setup. She had a vivid imagination.

Too vivid, she decided, certain every man on the street was watching her—eyeing her with lecherous intent.

At last she found the warehouse, and began searching for a safe place to park.

Although there were a few empty spots along the street, she doubted parking there would be safe. She'd be lucky if she had any hubcaps when she came out. Or a car, for that matter. Judicially, she opted for the attended parking lot two buildings down.

"Be long?" the attendant asked when she pulled in.

"An hour. Two at the most," she answered. She wanted to be back in her office by three at the latest and out of there by five. Tonight she and her roommate were going to have a talk. A long talk.

The parking attendant motioned for her to take a spot near the wall. She decided to call her office on her car phone before she got out, just in case her luck had changed and Asante had called at the last minute and canceled. Walking these streets purely for the exercise didn't appeal to her.

Waiting for the call to go through, she checked her makeup in the rearview mirror and patted her hair, pushing a stray piece back into place. She wished she weren't wearing her red suit. This was one day she didn't want to be noticed. At least not by the men around here.

"Any messages?" she asked when her secretary answered.

"Just one. From someone named Charlie. He said you'd know who he was?"

"Charlie?" Ashley tried to remember anyone named Charlie whom she'd met since moving to Chicago, then the name clicked. "Charlie Iler? From Ann Arbor?"

"He didn't say," her secretary answered. "All he said was you'd asked him to call if anything happened, and that he wasn't sure if anything had, but there was something on the news about a police raid Saturday night and people being shot, and he hadn't seen someone named Eric. Not for two days. That make any sense to you?"

"Yes," Ashley said numbly.

She didn't remember thanking her secretary or hanging up. Her next two calls were to Ann Arbor, the first to Eric's number, the second to Charlie's. When neither answered, she didn't know what to do.

She kept telling herself not to worry, that Eric was fine, that he could take care of himself. But the words didn't ease the pressure in her chest or take away the knot in her stomach. She'd told Charlie to call if anything happened to Eric.

And Charlie had called.

Her first impulse was to drive straight to Ann Arbor, and she had her hand on the ignition key before she realized she couldn't just take off. She was scheduled to meet with a client in five minutes, an important client. Maybe she could get a message to him by phone, but the idea seemed ridiculous when he wasn't that far away. She would go see him, apologize

and say something had come up, then she'd stop by
the office, put in for a couple days of vacation, and
take off. She'd be in Ann Arbor before five.

She left her briefcase in the car, locked up, and
started toward the warehouse. All she could think
about was Charlie's message. Just Friday night she'd
talked to Eric. He hadn't said anything about working
with the police. But then, he wouldn't have.

No, damn him. That part of his life was all hush-
hush.

Was he dead? The fear inside of her grew worse
with each step she took.

Was he lying in some hospital, too hurt to contact
anyone?

A narrow alleyway ran between the two buildings
close to the parking lot. She didn't even glance down
the shadowy space. Her thoughts were in Ann Arbor,
on Eric. It wasn't until she'd walked three or four steps
beyond the alley that she sensed she was no longer
alone.

By then it was too late.

It was four-thirty when Ashley entered the office
of Ronald Stedfeld. She knew her suit was a mess, the
jacket pocket torn and a button missing, that her hair
was disheveled, and in general she looked as though
she'd been through a war.

She didn't care.

He looked up from the note he was writing, then
frowned and set down his pen. "What happened to
you?"

"I ran into some trouble on my way to meet one of my clients. A man attacked me."

"You're okay?" Stedfeld stood, quickly scanning her from her mussed hair to the scuffed toes of her red pumps. "Sit down."

"I'm okay." But she did sit. It had been a long, draining afternoon. "I've been in a police station for the last three hours. They were going to book me for use of undue force."

She couldn't believe it. Eric had warned them in class, but she hadn't taken him seriously. After all, she was a woman. She didn't go out and start fights. If she used what he was teaching her, it would be because she needed to.

"Use of undue force?" Stedfeld repeated, the lines across his forehead deepening.

She laughed ruefully. "That means I hurt the guy more than he hurt me."

Still frowning, Stedfeld sat down, and Ashley explained. "I was in the warehouse district, on my way to a meeting with Dean Asante. He's the owner of Asante Sales. I'd just passed an alleyway when this guy came out and grabbed me from behind. I didn't think, just reacted the way Eric trained me. Except this time it was for real, and the police said that because I dislocated the guy's knee, broke his arm, and kneed him in the groin, I used undue force."

"You broke some guy's knee and arm?"

Stedfeld didn't sound as if he believed her. The two officers first on the scene hadn't believed it either, not until she said that she'd had some lessons in self-defense. That was when the guy who attacked her started yelling that she'd used undue force and threatened to sue her.

"It's what I was trained to do," she said matter-of-factly, realizing that having a taskmaster for an instructor had paid off.

"I don't believe it." Stedfeld continued to look worried. "I mean, they did drop that charge, didn't they?"

Ashley knew what was bothering him. A Stedfeld employee booked for undue force wouldn't be good for the company's image. "They dropped the charge, but only after we were at the station and another officer recognized my quote 'alleged assailant' as an escaped convict who had raped and brutally beaten three women in the past. He convinced the guy that he wouldn't have much of a case against me. That's when they said I could leave."

"Well, that's good." Once again Stedfeld looked her over. "You're sure you're all right? You're not going to file for workman's comp, are you?"

"No." She smiled. Did Stedfeld really care? No. With him it was always the image and how much it would cost.

Not that it mattered. Physically, she was fine. Emotionally, however, she was in a frenzy. She still didn't know what had happened to Eric.

"Well, then . . ." Stedfeld glanced down at the papers on his desk, and she knew he considered their conversation ended.

She didn't. "I do, however, need a couple of days off."

He looked surprised, and for a second she thought he'd say no. He nodded instead.

Eric parked his car in the lot across from the apartment building and grabbed his bag. As much as he'd enjoyed spending the weekend with his friend John, it was good to be back. And if he called right away, it wouldn't be too late to talk to Ashley, tell her about his trip. Not that she'd understand why two grown men would enjoy spending a couple of nights sleeping under the stars when it was 30 degrees out.

No, she probably wouldn't understand . . . but it would be good to talk to her.

And maybe he'd tell her he'd gotten a positive response to one of the feelers he'd sent to the colleges around Chicago. Or, then again, he might just wait until he had everything firmed up and could tell her he would be moving to the Chicago area.

Closing the dojo in Ann Arbor would be hard for him, both financially and emotionally, but things would work out. He had enjoyed teaching the two classes in Japanese culture that he'd given at the University of Michigan a couple of years ago. Teaching full time might be all right. And if in Tokyo the grand master could pass on the art of ninjitsu in a spare room, with no more than individual mats to work on, he could do the same in Chicago.

He stopped in the lobby to pick up his mail, stuffed it into his bag, then started up the stairs. Before he was halfway up, Charlie opened the door to the second-floor landing. The moment he saw

Eric, Charlie stopped, his mouth gaping open. He quickly closed it and looked back the way he'd come.

When he again looked at Eric, he was smiling. "You're home."

"And glad to be home, Charlie-san." Eric continued up the steps, then stopped beside Charlie. "I want to call Ashley before it gets too late, but tomorrow remind me to tell you about my weekend in the wilderness."

Still smiling, Charlie glanced at the door to Eric's apartment. "Oh, I'll want to hear about everything."

He started whistling as he went down the stairs, and Eric wondered what the man was up to. His curiosity grew as he neared his apartment. His door was half-open, and *koto* music was playing on his stereo.

Cautiously, he stepped into his apartment, then stopped. Ashley sat on his couch, slumped forward, elbows on her knees and her forehead cradled in her hands. Her hair was mussed, part up in a twist, but most loose and falling around her face, hiding her features.

The red of her suit was a contrast to the black leather of his couch, and he remembered the night she'd worn that suit to dinner . . . and how he'd taken it off her. He quietly closed his door, the click barely audible.

Nevertheless, Ashley heard it.

Straightening, she turned toward him. "Charlie, I was thinking—"

She stopped abruptly, and with a gasp rose to her feet. "Eric! Are you all right? I . . . We . . ."

He dropped his bag as she hurried across the room toward him, and his arms went around her as hers went around him. For two-and-a-half months he'd lived on phone calls and memories. Holding her, feeling her softness and warmth, was heaven. He didn't know why she was there, but he was glad to see her.

"Oh, Eric," she cried, hugging him. Then she abruptly loosened her hold and pulled back. Her expression concerned, she looked him up and down. "You are all right, aren't you? Not hurt anywhere?"

"I am fine." He chuckled. "It was primitive, but not dangerous."

"You're saying guns aren't dangerous?" she snapped, no longer soft but prickly.

"We did not take any guns. It was simply a camping trip."

"Camping?" She frowned.

"Up at Grayling. One of my students, John Rayburn, has been telling me how beautiful it is there, so on the spur of the moment, we decided to go. Why?"

"Why?" she asked, and laughed, the sound strained. "I'll tell you why. I've just spent the last eight, no nine, hours worrying myself sick about you, picturing you shot and dying. I've called every hospital in Ann Arbor, and Charlie's down in his apartment right now, getting a Detroit phone book so we can call those hospitals. And now you're telling me you've been camping?"

"Why would you think I was shot and dying?" He was certain he was missing something.

She left him, walking back to the couch where she picked up a newspaper from one of the cushions. She waved it in the air, then brought it to him. "This is why."

The headline was bold. POLICE RAID ENDS IN SHOOT-OUT. Taking the paper from her, Eric scanned the story, getting the basics. "And you thought I was there?" he asked, handing it back to her.

"Yes. What else was I to think? Lieutenant Pease calls, a ninja slips into the shadows, and a drug ring is broken up. If you'll recall, it happened right after I moved to Chicago . . . right after you got that one call. And maybe you can say there's no danger, but I know better. You've told me yourself, being a ninja doesn't make you invincible. Or immortal. You could have been one of the ones shot."

"Only if I'd been a part of that raid."

"But you, of course, were camping. Right?" She eyed him suspiciously, then shook her head. "You could drive me crazy, you know that, Eric Newman? Crazy."

Ashley tried to run her hand through her hair, only to snag her fingers where the twist held. Exasperated, she pulled out the remaining pins. "You know what I did when I first got here? I called Lieutenant Pease to find out how you were. And you know what some guy who answered the phone said? He said, 'I've never heard of a Lieutenant Pease.' That's what he said."

"You must have talked to someone new there. They have made a lot of changes lately."

"Right. So what happened to Pease?"

"Steve and his wife and two children moved to Connecticut the first of February. His wife's father is ill. They wanted to be closer to him."

"And who do you work with now?"

"No one." He smiled. "Ashley, I now truly do not do what I do not do."

She studied him in silence, then turned and walked back to the couch, dropping the paper on his coffee table as she sank down on a leather cushion. "So I worried for nothing." Shoulders slumped, she shook her head. "What a day!"

"What happened?" He'd already noticed the missing button and torn pocket of her jacket. It might be flattering to think she'd rent her clothing in worry for him, but he didn't believe that to be true.

She glanced back at him. "What happened? In the last twenty-four-hours, I've had a big argument with my father, came home to discover some couple I didn't even know making love in my bed, realized I don't like Chicago, thought you were dead, and was mugged."

"Mugged?"

She waved a hand, dismissing his concern. "It was nothing, other than all I wanted to do was get here and find out what had happened to you, and the police kept asking me the same stupid questions, over and over."

"You were mugged," he repeated, but she ignored him.

Knowing Eric was all right had lifted a weight from her shoulders. Other things now took precedence. Crucial things, like what was she going to do with the rest of her life? "Want to know what my father and I argued about?" she asked.

"I want to know what you mean by mugged," he said, walking over to the couch.

She dismissed his concern with a shrug. "A guy grabbed me; I got loose. That's what I mean. What my father and I argued about were goals and inequalities, stupid promises and guilt. You know what he said? He said I'm a fool for going to Chicago just because I thought it would make him happy. Here I work like a dog to please him, to make up for what I took away, and he says he wouldn't have done it, not if he'd been in my place. He said my living and working in Chicago didn't matter that much to him, that he just encouraged me because he didn't know what else to talk to me about. And I guess he was right. When I told him I didn't think Chicago was that great a place to live or work, he got angry, and we really didn't have anything else to talk about."

She sat back, remembering her disappointment. Long ago she'd accepted that her mother lived in a dreamworld. What a shock to realize her father was also clinging to dreams.

Chicago was his idea of paradise. He loved the town beyond reason, and even when he'd come to see her there, he'd seen only what he wanted to see—tall buildings, fancy storefronts, and elegant hotels, the hustle and bustle and the variety of entertainment. He'd missed the street people begging for money; the unsmiling faces of people locked into jobs they hated as much as he hated his; and the loneliness of the city.

"I come from one very dysfunctional family," she confessed. "My parents live in fantasy worlds, and I'm as bad as either of them. Here I am, twenty-seven years old, and only now am I seeing the truth."

"Ashley, do not be too harsh on yourself," Eric said, touching her hand.

"You know what the truth is?" she asked, and went on before he could answer. "The truth is, I hate working in Chicago, and I hate working at Stedfeld's. All the brownnosing and back-stabbing. It's not 'How can I help this client,' but 'How can this client help my career.' Everything is the bottom line. You know where I was happy?"

Eric said nothing, merely shook his head, but his eyes held understanding. And she knew he had always known where she belonged.

"I was happy here," she said. "In Ann Arbor. Here in this apartment building. Here people care. Maybe not everyone where I worked. Wayne and Jim were as bad as Stedfeld is. But Rod and Virginia and a lot of the others were great.

"And who could have had a better father than Charlie? Always watching out for me, worrying about me. Caring about my happiness. Or a better friend than you?"

Eric arched his eyebrows and glanced toward his bedroom. "Only a friend?"

She grinned. "All right. Friend *and* lover."

"So what are you going to do, my friend?" he asked, taking her hand.

"How would you feel if I came back here? To Ann Arbor?" Mentally, she crossed her fingers, hoping for a positive response.

She got it.

A smile slowly curved his mouth, and his gaze caressed her face. "That would be good. Very good."

"Maybe go into business on my own," she added. "Do free-lance public-relations work."

"It makes sense."

She hoped so. "Of course, I probably wouldn't make much money, not in the beginning, at least. But you know what? Money doesn't matter as much to me now." She squeezed his hand. "I have you to thank or blame for that."

"I am glad. And your promises?"

Ever since her talk with her father, she'd been thinking about that. "I promised Jack I would get a job in Chicago, that I'd do all he'd wanted to do. Well, I did it. He always said Stedfeld's was the best, and I made it to the top with them. He dreamed of a place where he'd have a view of Lake Michigan, and I lived in one."

Ashley played her fingertips over Eric's hand. "I lived the life he wanted. Now, it's time for me to live *my* life. No more promises, not to anyone."

He caught her fingers in his. "And what if I asked you to make a new promise?"

"Like what?" she asked cautiously.

"Like to love and cherish until death do us part."

Her concern melted in a surge of relief. A giddy sensation invaded her insides, and a silly smile spread over her face. "Sensei, that sounds a lot like a wedding vow."

"I would want a lifetime promise. A 'for richer and for poorer, in sickness and in health' commitment."

"Even with me coming from a crazy family and after I did something as crazy as leave you?"

"Perhaps I was crazy to let you go."

"No. You were wise." She'd needed to put her past behind her. Now, she was free to follow a new path, a path with Eric. "I'm just glad you didn't give up on me."

"Never." Lifting her hand to his lips, he kissed her fingers. "I think I have loved you since the day I first saw you, standing outside my door, your basket of wash on your hip."

She remembered. "With all of my underwear on top."

"Teasing me."

"You put me under your spell that night," she said. "I thought I could resist you, but I couldn't. I thought I could control my emotions, but even as I fought it, I was falling in love with you."

"You will marry me, then?"

"Of course."

"Of course," he repeated, then grinned and drew her close.

His kiss was possessive, his touch loving, and in his arms, she knew just how lonely she had been the past two-and-a-half months, how much she'd missed him. The lean, sinewy feel of his body, the strength of his arms, and the firm, demanding pressure of his mouth all made her feel complete. Wrapping her arms around him, she savored the wonder of him.

The first time she'd seen him, she'd known he was dangerous. What she hadn't realized was how exhilarating a little danger could be, how marvelous she would feel when the battle was over.

He slid his hands over her jacket, then laughed. "As usual, you have too many clothes on, Ashley-san."

"And, as usual, you'll do something about that, right?"

"Of course."

With his help she shrugged out of her jacket. "By the way," she said casually, watching it drop to the floor. "Sometime when you have a free minute, will you teach me how to incapacitate a man without breaking his arm?"

Eric frowned. "Without what?"

Grinning, she leaned close again. "Later," she murmured against his lips. "I'll explain later."

THE EDITOR'S CORNER

Summer is here at last, and we invite you to join us for our 11th anniversary. Things are really heating up with six wonderful new Loveswepts that sizzle with sexy heroes and dazzling heroines. As always, our romances are packed with tender emotion and steamy passion that are guaranteed to make this summer a hot one!

Always a favorite, Helen Mittermeyer gives us a heroine who is **MAGIC IN PASTEL,** Loveswept #690. When fashion model Pastel Marx gazes at Will Nordstrom, it's as if an earthquake hits him! Will desires her with an intensity that shocks him, but the anguish she tries to hide makes him want to protect her. Determined to help Pastel fight the demons that plague her, Will tries to comfort her, longing to know why his fairy-tale princess is imprisoned by her fear. Enveloped in the arms of a man whose touch soothes and arouses, Pastel struggles to accept the gift of his caring and keep their rare love true in a world of fire and ice. Helen delivers a story with characters that will warm your heart.

The heroine in Deborah Harmse's newest book finds herself **IN THE ARMS OF THE LAW**, Loveswept #691. Rebekah de Bieren decides Detective Mackenzie Hoyle has a handsome face, a great body, and a rotten attitude! When Mack asks Becky to help him persuade one of her students to testify in a murder case, he is stunned by this pint-sized blond angel who is as tempting as she is tough . . . but he refuses to take no for an answer—no matter how her blue eyes flash. Becky hears the sorrow behind Mack's cynical request and senses the tormented emotions he hides beneath his fierce dedication. Drawn to the fire she sees sparking in his cool gray eyes, she responds with shameless abandon—and makes him yearn for impossible dreams. Deborah Harmse will have you laughing and crying with this sexy romance.

FOR MEN ONLY, Loveswept #692, by the wonderfully talented Sally Goldenbaum, is a romance that cooks. The first time Ellie Livingston and Pete Webster met, he'd been a blind date from hell, but now he looks good enough to eat! Pete definitely has his doubts about taking a cooking class she's designed just for men, but his gaze is hungry for the pleasures only she can provide. Pete has learned not to trust beautiful women, but Ellie's smile is real—and full of temptation. Charmed by her spicy personality and passionate honesty, he revels in the sensual magic she weaves, but can Pete make her believe their love is enough? **FOR MEN ONLY** is a story you can really sink your teeth into.

Glenna McReynolds has given us another dark and dangerous hero in **THE DRAGON AND THE DOVE**, Loveswept #693. Cooper Daniels had asked for a female shark with an instinct for the jugular, but instead he's sent an angelfish in silk who looks too innocent to help him with his desperate quest to avenge his brother's death! Jessica Langston is fascinated by the hard sensuality of his face and mesmerized by eyes that meet hers with the force of a head-on collision, but she refuses to be dismissed—winning Cooper's respect and igniting his desire. Suddenly, Cooper is compelled by an inexorable need to claim her with tantalizing gentleness. Her surrender makes him yearn to rediscover the tenderness he's missed, but Cooper believes he'll only hurt the woman who has given him back his life. Jessica cherishes her tough hero, but now she must help heal the wounds that haunt his soul. **THE DRAGON AND THE DOVE** is Glenna at her heart-stopping best.

Donna Kauffman invites you to **TANGO IN PARADISE**, Loveswept #694. Jack Tango is devastatingly virile, outrageously seductive, and a definite danger to her peace of mind, but resort owner April Morgan needs his help enough to promise him whatever he wants—and she suspects what he wants is her in his arms! Jack wants her desperately but without regrets—and he'll wait until she pleads for his touch. April responds with wanton satisfaction to Jack's need to claim her soul, to possess and pleasure her, but even with him as her formidable ally, does she dare face old ghosts? **TANGO IN PARADISE** will show you why Donna is one of our brightest and fastest-rising stars.

Last, but definitely not least, is a battle of passion and will in Linda Wisdom's **O'HARA vs. WILDER**, Loveswept #695. For five years, Jake Wilder had been the man of her sexiest dreams, the best friend and partner she'd once dared to love, then leave, but seeing him again in the flesh leaves Tess O'Hara breathless . . . and wildly aroused! Capturing her mouth in a kiss that sears her to the toes and catches him in the fire-storm, Jake knows she is still more woman than any man can handle, but he is willing to try. Powerless to resist the kisses that brand her his forever, Tess fights the painful memories that their reckless past left her, but Jake insists they are a perfect team, in bed and out. Seduced by the electricity sizzling between them, tantalized beyond reason by Jake's wicked grin and rough edges, Tess wonders if a man who's always looked for trouble can settle for all she can give him. Linda Wisdom has another winner with **O'HARA vs. WILDER.**

Happy reading,

With warmest wishes,

Nita Taublib

Nita Taublib

Associate Publisher

P.S. Don't miss the women's novels coming your way in June—**WHERE SHADOWS GO,** by Eugenia Price, is an enthralling love story of the Old South that is the second volume of the *Georgia Trilogy*, following **BRIGHT CAPTIVITY; DARK JOURNEY,** by award-winning Sandra Canfield, is a heart-wrenching story of love and obsession, betrayal and forgiveness, in which a woman discovers the true price of forbidden passion; **SOMETHING BORROWED, SOMETHING BLUE,** by Jillian Karr, is a mixture of romance and suspense in which four brides—each with a dangerous secret—will be the focus of a deliciously glamorous issue of *Perfect Bride* magazine; and finally **THE MOON RIDER,** Virginia Lynn's most appealing historical romance to date, is a passionate tale of a highwayman and his ladylove. We'll be giving you a sneak peek at these wonderful books in next month's LOVESWEPTs. And immediately following this page look for a preview of the terrific romances from Bantam that are *available now!*

Don't miss these fantastic books by your favorite Bantam authors

On sale in April:

DECEPTION
by *Amanda Quick*

RELENTLESS
by *Patricia Potter*

SEIZED BY LOVE
by *Susan Johnson*

WILD CHILD
by *Suzanne Forster*

THE NEW YORK TIMES BESTSELLING NOVEL

DECEPTION
by *Amanda Quick*

"One of the hottest and most prolific writers in romance today . . . Her heroines are always spunky women you'd love to know and her heroes are dashing guys you'd love to love."
—USA Today

**NOW AVAILABLE IN PAPERBACK
WHEREVER BANTAM BOOKS ARE SOLD**

RELENTLESS

*Beneath the outlaw's smoldering gaze, Shea Randall felt
a stab of pure panic . . . and a shiver of shocking desire.
Held against her will by the darkly handsome bandit,
she knew that for her father's sake she must find a
way to escape. Only later, as the days of her captivity
turned into weeks and Rafe Tyler's fiery passion sparked
her own, did Shea fully realize her perilous position—
locked in a mountain lair with a man who could steal
her heart . . .*

The door opened, and the bright light of the
afternoon sun almost blinded her. Her eyes were
drawn to the large figure in the doorway. Silhou-
etted by the sun behind him, Tyler seemed even
bigger, stronger, more menacing. She had to force
herself to keep from backing away.

He hesitated, his gaze raking over the cabin,
raking over her. He frowned at the candle.

She stood. It took all her bravery, but she stood,
forcing her eyes to meet his, to determine what was
there. There seemed to be nothing but a certain
coolness.

"I'm thirsty," she said. It came out as more of a challenge than a request, and she saw a quick flicker of something in his eyes. She hoped it was remorse, but that thought was quickly extinguished by his reply.

"Used to better places?" It was a sneer, plain and simple, and Shea felt anger stirring again.

"I'm used to gentlemen and simple . . . humanity."

"That's strange, considering your claim that you're Randall's daughter."

"I haven't claimed anything to you."

"That's right, you haven't," he agreed in a disagreeable voice. "You haven't said much at all."

"And I don't intend to. Not to a thief and a traitor."

"Be careful, Miss Randall. Your . . . continued health depends on this thief and traitor."

"That's supposed to comfort me?" Her tone was pure acid.

His gaze stabbed her. "You'll have to forgive me. I'm out of practice in trying to comfort anyone. Ten years out of practice."

"So you're going to starve me?"

"No," he said slowly. "I'm not going to do *that*."

The statement was ominous to Shea. "What are you going to do?"

"Follow my rules, and I won't do anything."

"You already are. You're keeping me here against my will."

He was silent for a moment, and Shea noted a muscle moving in his neck, as if he were just barely restraining himself.

"Lady, because of your . . . father, I was 'held'

against my will for ten years." She wanted to slap him for his mockery. She wanted to kick him where it would hurt the most. But now was not the time.

"Is that it? You're taking revenge out on me?"

The muscle in his cheek moved again. "No, Miss Randall, it's not that. You just happened to be in the wrong place at the wrong time. I don't have any more choices than you do." He didn't know why in the hell he was explaining, except her last charge galled him.

"You do."

He turned away from her. "Believe what you want," he said, his voice indifferent. "Blow out that candle and come with me if you want some water."

She didn't want to go with him, but she was desperate to shake her thirst. She blew out the candle, hoping that once outside he wouldn't see dried streaks of tears on her face. She didn't want to give him that satisfaction.

She didn't have to worry. He paid no attention to her, and she had to scurry to keep up with his long-legged strides. She knew she was plain, especially so in the loose-fitting britches and shirt she wore and with her hair in a braid. She also knew she should be grateful that he was indifferent to her, but a part of her wanted to goad him, confuse him . . . attract him.

Shea felt color flood her face. To restrain her train of thought, she concentrated on her surroundings.

Her horse was gone, although her belongings were propped against the tree stump. There was a shack to the left, and she noticed a lock on the door. That must be where he'd taken the weapons and where he kept his own horse. The keys must be in his pockets. He strode over to the building and picked up a bucket with his gloved hand.

She tried to pay attention to their route, but it seemed they had just melted into the woods and everything looked alike. She thought of turning around and running, but he was only a couple of feet ahead of her.

He stopped abruptly at a stream and leaned against a tree, watching her.

She had never drunk from a stream before, yet that was obviously what he expected her to do. The dryness in her mouth was worse, and she couldn't wait. She moved to the edge of the stream and kneeled, feeling awkward and self-conscious, knowing he was watching and judging. She scooped up a handful of water, then another, trying to sip it before it leaked through her fingers. She caught just enough to be tantalized.

She finally fell flat on her stomach and put her mouth in the water, taking long swallows of the icy cold water, mindless of the way the front of her shirt got soaked, mindless of anything but water.

It felt wonderful and tasted wonderful. When she was finally sated, she reluctantly sat up, and her gaze went to Tyler.

His stance was lazy but his eyes, like fine emeralds, were intense with fire. She felt a corresponding wave of heat consume her. She couldn't move her gaze from him, no matter how hard she tried. It was as if they were locked together.

He was the first to divert his gaze and his face settled quickly into its usual indifferent mask.

She looked down and noticed that her wet shirt clung to her, outlining her breasts. She swallowed hard and turned around. She splashed water on her face, hoping it would cool the heat suffusing her body.

She kept expecting Tyler to order her away, but he didn't. And she lingered as long as she could. She didn't want to go back to the dark cabin. She didn't want to face him, or those intense emotions she didn't understand.

She felt his gaze on her, and knew she should feel fear. He had been in prison a very long time. But she was certain he wouldn't touch her in a sexual way.

Because he despises you.

Because he despises your father.

She closed her eyes for a moment, and when she opened them, a spiral of light gleamed through the trees, hitting the stream. She wanted to reach out and catch that sunbeam, to climb it to some safe place.

But there were no safe places any longer.

She watched that ray of light until it slowly dissipated as the sun slipped lower in the sky, and then she turned around again. She hadn't expected such patience from Tyler.

"Ready?" he asked in his hoarse whisper.

The word held many meanings.

Ready for what? She wasn't ready for any of this.

But she nodded.

He sauntered over and offered his hand.

She refused it and rose by herself, stunned by how much she suddenly wanted to take his hand, to feel that strength again.

And Shea realized her battle wasn't entirely with him. It was also with herself.

SUSAN JOHNSON

Nationally bestselling author of **Outlaw**
and **Silver Flame**

SEIZED BY LOVE

Now available in paperback

*Sweeping from the fabulous country estates and hunting
lodges to the opulent ballrooms and salons of the Russian
nobility, here is a novel of savage passions and dangerous
pleasures by the incomparable Susan Johnson, mistress of
the erotic historical.*

"*Under your protection?*" Alisa sputtered, flush-
ing vividly as the obvious and unmistakable clarity
of his explanation struck her. Of course, she should
have realized. How very stupid of her. The full
implication of what the public reaction to her
situation would be left her momentarily stunned,
devoured with shame. She was exceedingly thankful,
for the first time since her parents' death, that
they *weren't* alive to see the terrible depths to
which she had fallen, the sordid fate outlined for
her.

Irritated at the masterful certainty of Nikki's
assumption, and resentful to be treated once more

like a piece of property, she coldly said, "I don't recall placing myself under your protection."

"Come now, love," Nikki said reasonably, "if you recall, when I found you in that shed, your alternatives were surely limited; more severe beatings and possibly death if Forseus had continued drugging you. Hardly a choice of options, I should think. And consider it now," Nikki urged amiably, "plenty of advantages, especially if one has already shown a *decided* partiality for the man one has as protector. I'm not considered ungenerous, and if you contrive to please me in the future as well as you have to this date, we shall deal together quite easily."

Taking umbrage at his arrogant presumption that her role was to please *him*, Alisa indignantly said, "I haven't any *decided* partiality for you, you arrogant lecher, and furthermore—"

"Give me three minutes alone with you, my dear," Nikki interjected suavely, "and I feel sure I can restore my credit on that account."

Her eyes dropped shamefully before his candid regard, but she was angry enough to thrust aside the brief feeling of embarrassment, continuing belligerently. "Maria has some money of mine she brought with us. I'm not in *need* of protection."

"Not enough to buy you one decent gown, let alone support yourself, a child, and three servants," Nikki disagreed bluntly with his typical disregard for tact.

"Well, then," Alisa insisted heatedly, "I'm relatively well educated, young, and strong. I can obtain a position as governess."

"I agree in principle with your idea, but unfortunately, the pressures of existence in this world of travail serve to daunt the most optimistic hopes." His words were uttered in a lazy, mocking drawl. "For you, the role of governess"—the sarcasm in his voice was all too apparent—"is quite a pleasant conceit, my dear. You *will* forgive my speaking frankly, but I fear you are lacking in a sense of the realities of things.

"*If*—I say, *if*—any wife in her right mind would allow a provokingly beautiful young woman like yourself to enter her household, I'd wager a small fortune, the master of that house would be sharing your bed within the week. Consider the folly of the notion, love. At least with me there'd be no indignant wife to throw you and your retinue out into the street when her husband's preferences became obvious. And since I have a rather intimate knowledge of many of these wives, I think my opinion is to be relied upon. And as your protector," he continued equably, "I, of course, feel an obligation to maintain your daughter and servants in luxurious comfort."

"I am not a plaything to be bought!" Alisa said feelingly.

"Ah, my dear, but you are. Confess, it is a woman's role, primarily a pretty plaything for a man's pleasure and then inexorably as night follows day—a mother. Those are the two roles a woman plays. It's preordained. Don't fight it," he said practically.

Alisa would have done anything, she felt at that moment, to wipe that detestable look of smugness from Nikki's face.

"Perhaps I'll take Cernov up on his offer after all," she said with the obvious intent to provoke. "Is he richer than you? I must weigh the advantages if

I'm to make my way profitably in the demimonde," she went on calculatingly. "Since I'm merely a plaything, it behooves me to turn a practical frame of mind to the role of demirep and sell myself for the highest price in money and rank obtainable. I have a certain refinement of background—"

"Desist in the cataloguing if you please," he broke in rudely, and in a dangerously cold voice murmured, "Let us not cavil over trifles. You're staying with me." Alisa involuntarily quailed before the stark, open challenge in his eyes, and her heart sank in a most unpleasant way.

"So my life is a trifle?" she whispered, trembling with a quiet inner violence.

"You misunderstand, my dear," the even voice explained with just a touch of impatience. "It's simply that I don't intend to enter into any senseless wrangles or debates over your attributes and the direction in which your favors are to be bestowed. Madame, you're to remain my mistress." His lips smiled faintly but the smile never reached his eyes.

WILD CHILD
by Suzanne Forster
bestselling author of
SHAMELESS

"A storyteller of incandescent brilliance . . . beyond compare in a class by herself . . . that rare talent, a powerhouse writer whose extraordinary sensual touch can mesmerize . . ."
—*Romantic Times*

Her memorable characters and sizzling tales of romance and adventure have won her numerous awards and countless devoted readers. Now, with her trademark blend of intense sensuality and deep emotion, Suzanne Forster reunites adversaries who share a tangled past—and for whom an old spark of conflict will kindle into a dangerously passionate blaze . . .

"I want to talk about us," he said.

"Us?"

Blake could have predicted the stab of panic in her eyes, but he couldn't have predicted what was happening inside Cat. As she met his gaze, she felt herself dropping, a wind-rider caught in a powerful downdrift. The plummeting sensation in her stomach was sudden and sharp. The dock seemed to go out from under her feet, and as she imagined herself falling, she caught a glimpse of something in her mind that riveted her.

Surrender.

Even the glimpse of such naked emotion was terrifying to Cat. It entranced and enthralled her. It was the source of her panic. It was the wellspring of her deepest need. To be touched, to be loved. She shuddered in silence and raised her face to his.

By the time he did touch her, the shuddering was deep inside her. It was emotional and sexual and beautiful. No, she thought, this is impossible. This isn't happening. *Not with this man. Not with him . . .*

He curved his hand to her throat and drew her to him.

"What do I do, Cat?" he asked. "How do I make the sadness go away?"

The question rocked her softly, reverberating in the echo chamber her senses had become. *Not this man. Not him. He's hurt you too much. . . .*

"Sweet, sad, Cat." He caressed the underside of her chin with long, long strokes of his thumb. The sensations were soft and erotic and thrilling, and they accomplished exactly what they were supposed to, Cat realized, bringing her head up sharply. He wanted her to look up at him. He wanted her throat arched, her head tilted back.

No, Cat! He's hurt you too much.

"Don't," she whispered. "Not you . . ."

"Yes, Cat, me," he said. "It has to be me."

He bent toward her, and his lips touched hers with a lightning stroke of tenderness. Cat swallowed the moan in her throat. In all her guilty dreams of kissing Blake Wheeler—and there had been many—she had never imagined it as tender. She never had imagined a sweetness so sharp that it would fill her throat and tear through her heart like a poignant memory. Was this how lovers kissed? Lovers who had hurt each other and now needed to be very, very cautious? Lovers whose wounds weren't healed?

Age-old warnings stirred inside her. She should have resisted, she wanted to resist, but as his lips brushed over hers she felt yearnings flare up inside her—a wrenchingly sweet need to deepen the kiss, to be held and crushed in his arms. She had imagined him as self-absorbed, an egotistical lover who would take what he wanted and assume that being with him was enough for any woman. A night with Blake Wheeler. A night in heaven! She had imagined herself rejecting him, ordering him out of her bed and out of her life. She had imagined all of those things so many times . . . but never *tenderness*.

His mouth was warm. It was as vibrant as the water sparkling around them. She touched his arm, perhaps to push him away, and then his lips drifted over hers, and her touch became a caress. Her fingers shimmered over heat and muscle, and she felt a sudden, sharp need to be closer.

All of her attention was focused on the extraordinary thing that was happening to her. A kiss, she told herself, *it was just a kiss*. But he touched her with such rare tenderness. His fingers plucked at her nerve-strings as if she were a delicate musical instrument. His mouth transfused her with fire and drained her of energy at the same time. And when at last his arms came around her and brought her up against him, she felt a sweet burst of physical longing that saturated her senses.

She had dreamt of his body, too. And the feel of him now was almost more reality than she could stand. His thighs were steel, and his pelvic bones dug into her flesh. He was hard, righteously hard, and even the slightest shifts in pressure put her in touch with her own keening emptiness.

His tongue stroked her lips, and she opened

them to him slowly, irresistibly. On some level she knew she was playing a sword dance with her own emotions, tempting fate, tempting heartbreak, but the sensations were so exquisite, she couldn't stop herself. They seemed as inevitable and sensual as the deep currents swaying beneath them.

The first gliding touch of his tongue against hers electrified her. A gasp welled in her throat as he grazed her teeth and tingled sensitive surfaces. The penetration was deliciously languid and deep. By the time he lifted his mouth from hers, she was shocked and reeling from the taste of him.

The urge to push him away was instinctive.

"No, Cat," he said softly, inexplicably, "it's mine now. The sadness inside you is mine."

Studying her face, searching her eyes for something, he smoothed her hair and murmured melting suggestions that she couldn't consciously decipher. They tugged at her sweetly, hotly, pulling her insides to and fro, eliciting yearnings. Cat's first awareness of them was a kind of vague astonishment. It was deep and thrilling, what was happening inside her, like eddying water, like the sucking and pulling of currents. She'd never known such oddly captivating sensations.

The wooden dock creaked and the bay swelled gently beneath them, tugging at the pilings. Cat sighed as the rhythms of the sea and the man worked their enchantment. His hands *were* telepathic. They sought out all her tender spots. His fingers moved in concert with the deep currents, stroking the sideswells of her breasts, arousing her nerves to rivulets of excitement.

"Wild," he murmured as he cupped her breasts in his palms. "Wild, wild child."

And don't miss these spectacular
romances from Bantam Books,
on sale in May:

DARK JOURNEY
by the bestselling author
Sandra Canfield
"(Ms. Canfield's) superb style of writing
proves her to be an author extraordinaire."
—*Affaire de Coeur*

SOMETHING BORROWED
SOMETHING BLUE
by
Jillian Karr
"Author Jillian Karr . . . explodes onto the
mainstream fiction scene . . . Great reading."
—*Romantic Times*

THE MOON RIDER
by the highly acclaimed
Virginia Lynn
"A master storyteller."
—*Rendezvous*

SWP 7/93

Bestselling Women's Fiction

Sandra Brown

_____ 28951-9 TEXAS! LUCKY .... $5.99/6.99 in Canada
_____ 28990-X TEXAS! CHASE $5.99/6.99
_____ 29500-4 TEXAS! SAGE $5.99/6.99
_____ 29085-1 22 INDIGO PLACE $5.99/6.99
_____ 29783-X A WHOLE NEW LIGHT $5.99/6.99
_____ 56045-X TEMPERATURES RISING $5.99/6.99
_____ 56274-6 FANTA C $4.99/5.99
_____ 56278-9 LONG TIME COMING $4.99/5.99

Amanda Quick

_____ 28354-5 SEDUCTION $5.99/6.99
_____ 28932-2 SCANDAL $5.99/6.99
_____ 28594-7 SURRENDER $5.99/6.99
_____ 29325-7 RENDEZVOUS $5.99/6.99
_____ 29316-8 RECKLESS $5.99/6.99
_____ 29316-8 RAVISHED $4.99/5.99
_____ 29317-6 DANGEROUS $5.99/6.99
_____ 56506-0 DECEPTION $5.99/7.50

Nora Roberts

_____ 29078-9 GENUINE LIES $5.99/6.99
_____ 28578-5 PUBLIC SECRETS $5.99/6.99
_____ 26461-3 HOT ICE $5.99/6.99
_____ 26574-1 SACRED SINS $5.99/6.99
_____ 27859-2 SWEET REVENGE $5.99/6.99
_____ 27283-7 BRAZEN VIRTUE $5.99/6.99
_____ 29597-7 CARNAL INNOCENCE $5.50/6.50
_____ 29490-3 DIVINE EVIL $5.99/6.99

Iris Johansen

_____ 29871-2 LAST BRIDGE HOME $4.50/5.50
_____ 29604-3 THE GOLDEN BARBARIAN $4.99/5.99
_____ 29244-7 REAP THE WIND $4.99/5.99
_____ 29032-0 STORM WINDS $4.99/5.99
_____ 28855-5 THE WIND DANCER $4.95/5.95
_____ 29968-9 THE TIGER PRINCE $5.50/6.50
_____ 29944-1 THE MAGNIFICENT ROGUE $5.99/6.99
_____ 29945-X BELOVED SCOUNDREL $5.99/6.99

Ask for these titles at your bookstore or use this page to order.

Please send me the books I have checked above. I am enclosing $ _____ (add $2.50 to cover
postage and handling). Send check or money order, no cash or C. O. D.'s please.

Mr./ Ms. _____

Address _____

City/ State/ Zip _____

Send order to: Bantam Books, Dept. FN 16, 2451 S. Wolf Road, Des Plaines, IL 60018

Please allow four to six weeks for delivery.

Prices and availability subject to change without notice. FN 16 - 4/94